I0517493

MORIARTY PARADIGM

BASED UPON THE STORIES AND CHARACTERS CREATED BY

SIR ARTHUR CONAN DOYLE

ELIMINATING THE POSSIBLE

INTRODUCING THE MORIARTY PARADIGM

EDITED BY ADRIAN MIDDLETON

Fringeworks

For
The Sherlock Street Irregulars

First Published in Great Britain in 2013 by
FRINGEWORKS LTD
ISBN: 978-1-90573-05-5

Copyright © 2013 Fringeworks Ltd

This edition published in 2014

Original cover design: Martin Reimann
Cover art: Darrel Bevan, with colorisation by Anna Higgins
Cover format: David R Shires/TheImageDesign
Interior format: Damon Cavalchini
Interior art: Darrel Bevan, Sidney Paget except for 'A Chase' - Illustrated
London News, 17th June 1865
Elements of this book use Birmingham and Eccentric fonts

All rights reserved. No part of this book may be reproduced in any form
or by any means, except by inclusion of brief quotations in a review, without
permission in writing from the publisher.

CONTENTS

INTRODUCTION

Holmes. Watson. Moriarty. These are names that conjure up images a different age, where the British Empire casts a long shadow over the rest of the world, while at home, in a gas-lit London on cobbled streets and horse-drawn carriages, gentlemen detectives foil the deceptive schemes of rakish villains, while the more gruesome crimes of the working classes are dealt with, efficiently but clumsily, by the fledgling inspectors of Scotland Yard.

While not the first detective, Sherlock Holmes was the most inspirational, and the most enduring. Whether Doyle intended it, he created characters whose flaws and foibles have been redefined by the passing generations, and whose methods, while unrealistic, became the model for the many great detectives who followed in his wake.

Moriarty, meanwhile, became the slow-burning archetype for the comic book criminal Mastermind. Vastly intelligent, exceedingly manipulative, and just a little unhinged. To Holmes he was the bogeyman, an antithesis whose sole function was to conclude the great detective's adventures and to effect his author's retirement from the journeyman detective stories that dogged his entire life.

Holmes, of course, was invented a century before the term 'steampunk' came into existence. When James Blaylock, K.W. Jeter and Tim Powers dabbled in the resurrection of the scientific romance their inspiration lay not within the detective genre, but within the the works of Doyle's more fantastical contemporaries, Burroughs, Griffith, Wells and Verne. And yet with the cultural rise of the steampunk aesthetic it has been the character of Sherlock Holmes that has most successfully brought the concept of steampunk into the mainstream. It was Stephen Spielberg's 1985 film *Young Sherlock Holmes and the Pyramid of Fear* that first captured that aesthetic, bringing much of the imagery from Tim Powers' *The Anubis Gates* to the big screen, and this transition continued into the twenty first century, when Guy Ritchie's *Sherlock Holmes* films reinvented both the character and the period for the modern audiences. In particular, the second of these, *Sherlock Holmes: Game of Shadows*, brought Holmes' high-octane adventures once more under the steampunk spotlight; and when followers of steampunk fashion say that 'Sherlock Holmes *is* steampunk', it is surely the duty of any writer to show them, and not to tell them, how wrong they are.

Here then, is the commencement of an education. If you like Sherlock Holmes but haven't quite grasped what steampunk is, then perhaps the

Moriarty paradigm will show you the difference; and if you are one of those steampunks who thinks Holmes is steampunk, but perhaps never got around to reading the original stories, then perhaps we can persuade you to think again.

Through these volumes we will be presenting both a series of mash-ups using the original Holmes canon, and an original series of short stories and novellas based upon the original Holmes canon. Unlike the originals, these stories really *are* steampunk, and the challenge of these tales is to read them, and then to return to the original stories by Doyle. This Sherlock Holmes *is* steampunk, but the original is not.

ADRIAN MIDDLETON, 2013
Birmingham, West Midlands

A Note from Doctor Doyle

In the age of scientific romance, Sir Arthur Conan Doyle had the opportunity to write science fiction adventure stories, and as his Professor Challenger series attests, they were as fantastical as any of the works of Verne or Wells. Had both steampunk and the modern crime novel existed when he was writing Holmes, perhaps he might have been prepared to cross the genres, and been more forgiving of the Great Detective and the impact he had upon Doyle's other writings. In a steampunk world, as friend and editor of John Watson, he might have had something to say:

There has, over the years, been considerable speculation about why, as a writer, I give Dr John H. Watson credit for the adventures of Sherlock Holmes. Similarly, the good doctor receives mail asking quite the opposite question, "Why, when it is clear you are the writer of these accounts, do you tolerate the credit being taken by Conan Doyle?"

The truth of the matter is that my friendship with Dr Watson is a long one, and that we have been acquainted for a good number of years, having attended medical school together in our younger days. After a stint at sea, I had ended up abandoning my ailing general practice to pursue a career in literature. Meanwhile, my good friend James had transferred to London where he trained as a surgeon before embarking upon a military career which took him away from England. He would ultimately distinguish himself as the Hero of Maiwand, a pivotal battle of the Second Afghan War, where his bravery and determination had seen him through one of the worst defeats ever suffered by the British Army.

I had not thought our paths would cross again, but they did so much sooner than expected. In the year 1882 I had set up a medical practice in Portsmouth which, by coincidence, was a major mooring town for military transport ships and aerostats. It was there, struggling to make my living as a doctor, that I again encountered Surgeon-Lieutenant James Watson.

Like many other survivors of the Afghan conflicts, Watson had been invalided home with wounds acquired in Maiwand. After disembarking he was transferred to a Southsea sanatorium where he was allowed to convalesce, and it was here that I briefly attended upon him as a locum doctor.

I barely recognised the frail, unshaven young man made gaunt by a recent bout of typhus. This, I had no doubt, had been caused by contaminated water in an Indian field hospital. His ruddy, tanned skin clung tightly to the contours of his skull in a way that would have rendered him a stranger to me, had he not called out my name and smiled at the appearance of a familiar face. The plump, clean shaven young man I had met as a freshman in Edinburgh was long gone, but in the weeks that followed I saw his complexion return, and his dysenteric symptoms abate. As he grew stronger I became a regular visitor to his bedside, where we exchanged tales of our respective adventures before, at last, he was discharged and ready to return to civilian life.

In the weeks we spent together I had confided in James that I was boosting my finances by writing fiction. He had joked that a literary career was better suited to me than a medical one, and insisted that I bring some of my work to read at his bedside. He was, he confessed, an amateur diarist himself, and shared with me the notes he had taken from his continental experiences. We discussed the idea that I should edit these notes, shaping them into a dramatic account of his short but eventful military experiences. While nothing came of it, I was privileged to hear his account of the Maiwand incident. He never spoke of it again, and its omission from his written memoirs suggest to me that it is not a place he would ever wish to revisit. I hope he can forgive me for recounting that experience here:

Watson had been attached to Major General 'Bob' Roberts' field force when it entered Afghanistan in retaliation for the massacre of the British administration in Kabul. He was soon assigned as medical officer aboard the relief aerostat *Keane*, where he spent much of his time above and behind the lines of military action. From the *Keane* he witnessed the defeat of the Afghan Army at Charasiab, and he was high above the Khyber Pass when he watched the British and Indian armies march into Kabul.

Shortly after the execution of the rebel leaders and installation of a new emir, the *Keane* was transferred to the Kandahar garrison. There, in May 1880, Watson learned of a revolt some fifty miles to the north west. Ayub Khan, the governor of Herat, had raised an Afghan army made up from hundreds of Ghazi warriors and thousands of local tribesmen. His goal was to expel the hated British from the region and to supplant Abdur Rahman as the Emir of Afghanistan.

In July of that year the *Keane* and a second rigid aerostat, the *Vigilant*, supported 2,500 men of the 66th Berkshire Regiment under the command of Brigadier General George Burrows. Six thousand Afghan soldiers accompanied them, but in the blistering summer heat there were many desertions, and the column suffered badly as it crossed the desert.

Aboard his aerostat, Surgeon-Major Watson survived the journey

relatively unscathed, spending much of his time tending to sufferers of heatstroke in the field ward that filled the rear of the *Keane*'s gondola.

It was on the 27th of July, at the Maiwand Pass, that disaster struck. While the *Keane* was giving medical and logistical support towards the rear of the column, the *Vigilant* was intended to provide reconnaissance and air cover beyond the range of the Afghan's muzzle-loading jezail rifles. Aerial spotters and crack unit of Bangalore sharpshooters manned its decks, ready to spot and pick off the enemy with their long-barrelled air guns.

Nobody knows how the *Vigilant* managed to miss the rebels hidden in the mountains. The British were quickly surrounded, outnumbered by a factor of ten to one, and heavily out-gunned. Aside from rumours and sightings of a few Afghan horsemen, General Burrows had been completely outflanked. More than twenty thousand Afghans, led by the white-robed Ghazi warriors and supported by a well-armed artillery and massed Afghan horsemen pressed forwards against the British and Indian line. Wave after wave came, quickly forcing a British retreat.

The war in the air fared no better. The *Vigilant* soon broke away to keep out of artillery range. According to its commanding officer, the renowned Colonel Bastian Moran, his sharpshooters were useless in the face of so many Afghans. Circling the

battlefield at a distance, it played little part in the conflict, other than to carry news back to Kandahar and to alert the garrison to Burrows' defeat.

The *Keane*, meanwhile, was struck by an incendiary shell even before the British and Afghan forces clashed. Watson himself had seen the tell-tail trail of blue smoke that indicated a burning phosphorous charge. Alerting the crew to the danger, it was Watson who released the *Keane*'s ballast, unbalancing the ship's trim and lifting her aloft. Instead of piercing the hydrogen-filled gas-bags it was made to ignite the shell, made by the Russians and supplied, along with the howitzers needed to fire them, to the Afghan army, struck the *Keane*'s lightly-armoured gondola amidships.

Nearly a dozen men were killed by the initial explosion, including the senior officer, Captain George Downing. Struck by fragments of wood and metal along the left side of his body, the injured Watson took command of the ship, ordering the pilot to turn and steer it clear of the battlefield.

There was still a small fire, but by the time it spread to the ship's main balloon, the *Keane* had limped away from Maiwand where, low to the ground and far from home, it erupted into flames somewhere over the Panjshir Valley.

Despite the chaos, the evacuation had been an orderly affair, and all that had survived the first attack gathered to take their orders from the Surgeon-

Major. As the senior surviving officer Watson led his men through the hostile Afghan mountains to arrive back at the Kandahar garrison fifteen days later.

In spite the praise for his actions, which were rightfully mentioned in despatches, Watson's account of the incident had been quite modest, and he expressed gratitude that he had not been stuck on the ground, where many Indian and British soldiers had been trampled underfoot, riddled with jezail bullets or cut to pieces by long Ghazi blades.

As a civilian, Watson returned to London, and while we maintained a perfunctory correspondence, our paths did not cross again until, in 1886, I was summoned to the offices of Ward & Lock at Salisbury Square. The appointment was with George Bettany, the editor of *Beeton's Christmas Annual*, but at his side sat my dear friend James Watson. It was here that our literary partnership was formed.

Watson explained that he had reduced his hours in medical practice to accommodate the launch of a new business venture with his partner, Mr Sherlock Holmes. Describing himself as a 'consulting detective', Holmes was struggling to secure work that paid well. He was either giving much of his time, free-of-charge, to the police, or else he was consulting without charging proper fees. James had struck upon the idea of writing up their more sensational cases as a means of promoting the business, and had set about getting his stories published. After attempting, unsuccessfully, to get his stories published in a number of periodicals including the *Cornhill*, for which I had myself written, he had turned to publishers such as Arrowsmiths, Warnes and, eventually, Ward & Lock. It was there, confronted with the feedback that a writer dreads—that his literary style was unsuitable for publication—that James had mentioned my name, and a compromise had been struck. If I would agree to edit and reinterpret Watson's notes for the princely sum of £25, I would receive the author's credit and a share of the royalties when the story was finally serialised.

It was a simple arrangement that I paid little heed to at the time, until Lippincott's Magazine, doubtless aware of Sherlock Holmes' growing reputation across London, approached me to write a second adventure. I could not, in all good conscience, produce a fictional sequel, and so I approached Watson and we stuck a long-term deal in which I would select the best cases for serialization, whilst helping Holmes and Watson to receive the worldwide recognition that their fledgling detective business so desperately required.

SIR ARTHUR CONAN
DOYLE, 1924

A CHASE
by Mike Chinn

In our second Holmes novel, the background events of Valley of Fear are transplanted to the Moon, where colonial workers prepare the way for the British Empire's future conquest of the solar system. Much of the action still takes place with Holmes and Watson's feet planted, most firmly, upon the Earth, but in a steampunk world, the action is more thrilling, and more pulse-pounding, as this excerpt from Mike Chinn proves, beyond any reasonable doubt:

At Holmes' insistence we awaited the dawn before leaving Birlstone Manor; and Mrs Allen would not let any of us leave without breakfasting to some degree. Indeed, Mrs Douglas had to be firm with the kindly housekeeper who was determined to ply us all with a full meal. Reluctantly, she agreed to pack some sandwiches for us—but would not be swayed over the provision of strong tea and coffee. Finally, refreshed if unshaven, we quit the manor grounds and headed towards the town's small railway station. Douglas submitted himself fully to the custody of Inspector MacDonald, whilst his determined wife—after many stubborn words—was allowed to accompany us. I admit to feeling a little wretched when I thought back over my immediate reactions to her, and how I had considered her in any way complicit in her husband's murder. She was, I now realised, an admirable woman: a credit to her fair sex, unswayable when in the right, and a staunch companion. Douglas was indeed the most fortunate of men. Barker also demanded to be allowed to accompany his friend, and none of us felt able to deny this forceful man.

Only on one point did the American and inspector disagree: Douglas insisted on carrying a large pistol—a repeater from his native shores—which carried its ammunition in a vertical box magazine attached just before the trigger guard. The guard itself formed part of a lever which cocked and armed the weapon—rather in the manner of a Winchester rifle—and altogether it seemed to me a bulky and unmanageable firearm; if not for a tailored pocket inside his coat, he would have been reduced to carrying it in his hand. MacDonald was, quite understandably, disinclined to allow a man—who was for all purposes his prisoner—to be armed, but after Holmes intervened, Douglas was allowed to retain the cannon.

"After all, Mr Mac," said Holmes, "are either you or Mr White Mason armed? Is Mr Barker? I know that neither Watson nor myself are."

The inspector's great brows drew down. "Armed? Man, are you saying we should be?"

My friend's expression was neutral, but I fancy I detected the faintest edge of unease about his eyes. "I trust that I am wrong, inspector—but it may be that Douglas's pistol will be of use to us before we reach London."

The railway station was a little under half a mile outside the tiny village. As we made our way towards it we encountered no other souls—shopkeepers yet abed, farmworkers in their fields well before first light—and perhaps it was as well. Six men and one woman, taking a stroll through the Surrey countryside at such an hour might engender more questions that we would comfortably answer. Douglas and his wife walked together, conferring intermittently and in low tones; Holmes, MacDonald, Barker, White Mason and I flanked them—yet not so close that we might eavesdrop on their desultory conversation. I believe none of us thought there was anything man or wife could say to our interest at this stage—and much it would be imprudent to overhear.

The station was deserted on our arrival. As we filed into the ticket-office, Holmes raised a commanding hand, holding us back as he walked through and thoroughly scrutinised the platform. Then a cursory gesture summoned us forward.

"I see there are seventeen minutes before the arrival of our train," spoke Holmes, gesturing at the wall-mounted timetable. "Perhaps, Mr Mac, it would be wise to have Mr and Mrs Douglas wait inside the stationmaster's office until then."

"What?" snapped Barker. "Is the man to be detained already?"

Homes shook his head. "Precautions, Mr Barker. Your friend has invested too much time and effort in maintaining his invisibility to squander the advantage."

Douglas took Barker's shoulder. "Let it go, Cecil," said he softly. "He has the right of it: it's too soon to be dropping my guard."

Barker harrumphed loudly, but allowed MacDonald to usher the Douglases into the stationmaster's cramped office, where at least they would have a cosy fire. Then White Mason, Barker, Holmes and I stood on the draughty platform, huddled into our coats; it looked as though it would be another sunny day—albeit a cold one. Holmes alone appeared unaffected by the weather; having lit one of his cannabis cigarettes while he waited.

"We must be alert," said he.

White Mason's cheerful expression never changed. "You're expecting trouble?"

"But why?" Barker drew up his collar and tugged at his hat-brim. "Baldwin is dead; the message sent out—"

Holmes grinned a skeletal smile. "Mr Barker, I believe we are dealing with men of the most mistrustful character. Suspicion is a way of life: of outsiders and most insidiously, of each other." He threw his finished cigarette towards the railway line below us. "Do you think that they would be content with something so simple as a note left with a body? It smacks of the melodramatic and has limited practicality. What if the note were lost, or overlooked? If some rustic bobby—and I mean no offence, Mr White Mason— trampled it to the floor, or tossed it aside, assuming it to be nothing? Or if it were simply not reported: an irrelevance carelessly annotated, and instantly dismissed from memory? How then would word get back?"

A tethered aerostat whined by overhead. We paused until the high-pitched drone conducted by the tethering cables dimmed; I took the time to collect my thoughts before speaking.

"The note was merely symbolic. A gesture. Baldwin—" and I found myself looking around the otherwise empty railway station uneasily "— would be expected to rendezvous with others of his kind."

"Hah! You have the gist of it, Watson! Once Baldwin had done his work he would flee—quite possibly by the very route you, Barker, suggested with your crude theatricals—"

A black scowl disfigured Barker's heavy face.

"—then he must meet up with a confederate at a time and a place pre-agreed upon, to report success. Only then would these hard, twisted minds accept Douglas's death. I'm afraid all of your friend's clever improvisations may only have delayed the inevitable, Barker. As with the Hydra of myth— cut off one head, another two will replace it!"

Barker appeared abruptly shrunken: his hard-eyed bravado punctured. "Then what must we do, Mr Holmes?"

"We are ahead in the game—by how much I know not—but that is our one advantage. Once Douglas is in London, and under the aegis of Scotland Yard, I believe our man will be safe enough."

We had been joined on the platform by more travellers. A pretty young woman who, to judge by her dress, was a member of the professional class; two men in shapeless overcoats and equally formless hats who looked like labourers or farm workers; and three more scarcely out of boyhood in sharp, modern suits—talking in excited, staccato voices and smoking endless cigarettes. From the distance came the shriek of a locomotive whistle, made sharp and brilliant by the cold air. Everyone except the labourers grew expectant at the sound: obviously through experience or knowledge of the timetable they had judged their arrival more expertly than our own.

White Mason consulted his watch—a huge sphere of a timepiece—and grunted with

satisfaction. "Perfectly on time. Shall I fetch Mr MacDonald and the Douglases?"

Holmes laid a restraining hand on his wrist. "Allow me, detective. Do you all board the train when it arrives and secure us a compartment. I shall join you presently." With that he left us on the platform and vanished inside the stationmaster's office.

The train arrived at the station, pulled I noted by one of the new compact turbine-electric locomotives; although only an 0-4-0+0-4-0, it was so much more efficient than the huge Reid-Ramsey prototypes from which all subsequent working locomotives derived. Its sleek, modern lines were in sharp contrast to the rake of ageing, clerestory-roofed carriages it hauled, and I wondered to what degree the designer had been influenced by the freight and passenger balloons which had become the railways' greatest competitor.

Barker quickly found an empty first-class compartment. White Mason and he settled themselves down whilst I stood by the door, looking towards the stationmaster's office and wondering where the deuce Holmes was. If they did not hurry he, MacDonald and the Douglases would miss the train entirely. The two labourers had made no effort to board the train: either meeting a passenger or awaiting some item of luggage, I assumed.

The guard blew his whistle, and Holmes was still nowhere to be seen. The carriage shuddered as the locomotive began to pull on its load, the only sound being the hiss of leaking steam. Barker was at my side—equally alarmed by events.

"Where are they?" he cried. "Has there been—?"

The office door flew wide; Holmes, the inspector and his charges appeared through it and sprinted across the narrow space of platform. Holmes tore the compartment door open and all four tumbled in—my friend last of all. He slammed the door shut behind him and laughed in what I considered an inappropriate delight.

"Most exhilarating! You must recommend such early-morning pursuits to your patients, Watson!"

"What was the meaning for such a display?" demanded Barker. He stood aside to allow Mrs Douglas to sit herself; her beautiful face was pale, but two bright spots burned high on her cheeks. Her husband seemed perplexed, whilst MacDonald stood gasping for breath. Holmes dropped open the window and looked towards the receding railway station before stepping back and pulling the window shut again.

"We have the drop on them, as you Americans say. I doubt they will be caught so easily a second time."

"Holmes," said I, "some kind of explanation, if you would be so kind?"

He laughed again, in high spirits after his sudden, violent exertion. "My apologies, friend Watson—I

had no opportunity to acquaint you with my likely actions; and there were too many ears to hear, besides. Let us all sit and recover ourselves." We joined Mrs Douglas and White Mason, Holmes sliding the window tightly shut.

Taking out his pipe, my friend packed it with tobacco and began to smoke in silence. Since it was obvious there would be no speedy explanation, I offered my own cigarettes—Douglas and MacDonald gratefully took one each—and we all waited on Holmes. The air of the compartment grew quite thick—thanks mostly to Holmes' ghastly tobacco which even the clerestory louvres failed to ventilate—and Mrs Douglas opened the window to allow the miasma to exit. Ashamed by the tacit rebuke, I extinguished my own half-smoked bird's eye, as did Douglas and the inspector; Holmes, however, puffed on oblivious, as he marshalled his thoughts before revealing them a capite ad calcem.

Eventually, he spoke. "You will, of course, have observed our fellow travellers on the platform this morning: the young lady Teslagraph operator, the labourers, and the three shop assistants out for a day in London to celebrate a birthday."

MacDonald winked in my direction with a laugh. "Ay, Mr Holmes—we all saw six other people waiting for the train."

"On the contrary, Mr Mac, you saw four awaiting this train—and two for Mr Douglas."

White Mason's broad face widened further with delight. "I'd be honoured if you'd share your reasoning with us, Mr Holmes."

My friend bowed his head at the compliment, taking full delight in it. He used the stem of his pipe to highlight his several points. "The girl removed her thick winter gloves for a few moments, to place a ticket in her reticule. I observed the mild spatulation on the fingertips of her right hand— an indication that she habitually depresses typing keys with that hand—but none on the left. However, there was a small burn across the back of that hand—a long and narrow cicatrice which might be caused by a hot wire. Hence she is not a typewritist—else both sets of fingertips would be broadened; Teslagraph operators have a small array of keys to tap, one-handed, whilst the small burn is typical of an occupational hazard amongst those new to the job: many Teslagraphs are often badly-earthed."

"Marvellous, Mr Holmes, marvellous." White Mason was clearly delighted; whilst I was pleased not to be cast in the role of Holmes' foil. "And I suppose you deduced the shop-boys by the ink under their nails?"

Holmes threw his head back and barked a short laugh. "Capital! You see, Watson, the dangers of your romanticised fictions? I am cast

forever as a Dupin who may fathom a person's role and motives from the creases in their trousers! Not at all, Mr White Mason, not at all. They were talking loudly enough for all to hear; I merely listened…"

It was my turn to smile. "Which leaves the labourers—who are, I imagine, anything but that?"

"They are certainly men used to the most gruelling of heavy labour, Watson. Life has beaten all softness from their flesh and hearts. But not in the fields that we know, I'll hazard. Their coats were big and shapeless, but not bulky enough to disguise the presence of the objects carried underneath, in poachers' pockets. Objects which by their dimensions suggested themselves to be more of your scowrers, Mr Douglas."

The American did not seem surprised: his reaction was muted. "My enemies are legion, Mr Holmes," said he with a trace of bitterness.

"In addition," continued Holmes, "even though their unsightly hats were jammed hard over their heads, I could still perceive tufts of badly-dyed hair. Hair which under the inexpertly smeared boot-blacking is as white as your own, Mr Douglas."

Barker leaned forward. "More of the dead Baldwin's stamp?"

"Precisely that. They have been awaiting word from their dead comrade—or a direct confirmation that Douglas is no more—I apologize for my directness, Mrs Douglas."

The admirable woman drew herself up, taking her husband's arm. "Not at all, Mr Holmes. I am grateful that you are so forthright."

He bowed his head. "Receiving neither word nor rendezvous they reasoned that Douglas lived still and would soon be fleeing Birlstone— most likely by train. And so—" here he paused again, his pale lips twitching "—they staked out the railway station. I believe that is the appropriate colloquialism, is it not? However, they arrived late on our heels, by which time Mr Mac had Mr and Mrs Douglas out of sight in the stationmaster's office. They could not be sure which train their prey might take but would, I am sure was the plan, board it the very moment they saw him embarking; and then finish what the wretched Baldwin had so obviously failed to do. Again, Mrs Douglas—"

She waved his apology aside.

"—by delaying as long as possible—until the train was already in motion—we caught them by surprise."

"So?" Mrs Douglas's eyes were liquid with hope. "We have escaped them?"

"For now, madam." Holmes glanced out of the compartment window; I realised he was watching the supports of the tethered aerostat lines as they flicked past. The humour passed instantly, and he reached for one of the paper-wrapped bundles Birlstone Manor's insistent housekeeper had pressed upon us. "However, let us now see what the estimable Mrs Allen has provided for our breakfast."

It was a crude repast: thickly-cut slices of bread smeared with salty butter and wrapped around lumps of sharp local cheese, some eggs the housekeeper had somehow found time to hard-boil, and slabs of pork pie. Nevertheless it was quite delicious; I had quite forgotten my hunger until the first bite—and then I fell upon the meal with a gluttonous appetite. In addition, a large sweet, crisp apple had been packed for each of us—no doubt from a store laid up for the winter months—which complemented the cheese perfectly. Holmes did the simple meal full justice; whilst our two policemen chewed on stoically with the detachment of those used to eating at irregular hours, and often poorly. Mrs Douglas picked at her own, taking bird-sized pecks from her apple whilst ignoring the rest; her husband gave all the appearance of a man forcing down damp wallpaper; and Barker tore his food to shreds as though offended by its rustic simplicity.

Once we were done, Holmes consulted his watch. "They will be coming soon, Watson," said he quietly, "and we are ill-prepared. Oh, for the gift of foresight—then should we have left London armed and ready!"

"How will they reach us?" I asked.

"Even should they in some wise steal a train or locomotive, short of ramming this one and risking all on board, they could not stop us."

He laughed—though there was little humour in it. "In truth, my friend, I would not consider such actions beyond them. They are past subtlety; their only goal now is success—at any price! But no: they have another course—and one that will be no real challenge for whatever skills they may have acquired on the Moon—"

The train shuddered into motionlessness and Holmes leapt for the door. Flinging it wide he stepped down onto a brief platform: the station—nameless as far as I could see—was little more than a halt. Seated as I was by the opened doorway, I could see exactly as did Holmes: no one either alighted or boarded. Moments later the locomotive sounded a shrill whistle and I stepped aside for Holmes to re-enter our compartment—though he leaned his thin frame through the window for many seconds, until the anonymous station was accelerating to the rear. Eventually satisfied upon some point, he extricated himself from the window frame and slid the glass up. Beckoning me closer, he lowered his voice to a more conspiratorial tone.

"That was the last stop before London. We might expect our enemies soon." He indicated the aerostat line running above us. "Pressed—taken to the fullest limit

of its speed—I believe one of those aerial freighters might overtake us."

I thought quickly. My experience of aerostats was limited to the larger species, and that the military kind. I understood that vessels such as the ill-fated HMAS Keane are capable of speeds in excess of seventy knots—though the full details are understandably kept secret by the government—whilst most aerial liners are content to cruise somewhere around the fifty mark. I could conceive of no reason why a tethered aerostat—its electric engines given full rein—should not match those performances. Only the restrictions placed on the machines by railway and canal companies preventing them from rocketing along their restraining cables at previously unheard of speed.

"Holmes—one could outpace this train, I'm sure. Particularly if any loaded freight were to be dumped…"

"Your thoughts accord with mine." He tapped a window, his fingers rapping out a staccato drumroll. Then he fell back against his seat, his lips quirking; his eyes twinkling with sudden mischief. "Well, we still have a lengthy journey before us," he said aloud, addressing the compartment in general, "and little to divert us beyond the English countryside in winter; therefore I feel it is time that I acquainted you with the true facts behind my good friend's melodramatic account of our recent cases. I have a fancy to one day set them down myself, recording the definitive interpretation of events— free of sentiment and emotional detour. To that end I must stimulate the muscles of a raconteur."

In all the years I have known Holmes, it would be fair to say I have never known him to be comfortable in the role of conversationalist: only when expounding on his deductions—and enjoying the fruits of his singular brain—was he anything but brusque or to the point. That morning, however, he had his small audience captive: contrasting my own—oft criticised—narrative style against what he considered the more authentic voice of the dealer in facts. Like a polished university lecturer he presented his case, assembled his facts and drew his conclusions, without once lapsing into pedantry; he even provoked an occasional smile or appreciative chuckle. In all, a praiseworthy performance; I only regret I was unable to record it verbatim—for I believe many have come to see my friend as a dry stick, with no room for frivolity in his difference engine of a heart. But I was occupied, surreptitiously watching out for our pursuers, as Holmes knew I would, whilst he distracted them.

I spotted the gaining aerostat easily: outlined against a clear sky, its rigid, mantle glinted in the winter Sun. The reception aerials by which it received its transmitted power were swept back at rakish angles—four in all; two on the dorsal surface, two on the ventral—providing it with a vaguely piscine appearance. It was still riding at regulation height as far as I could judge; but I knew the winches of these aerial freighters were capable of grounding a behemoth such as this in two minutes or less: speed and efficiency were the currency by which the several companies who owned the tethered air fleets thrived or perished.

I glanced towards Holmes. He interpreted my glance in a second and acknowledged with a terse nod. Then his speech became quick and urgent as he explained to all what was happening. Mrs Douglas's emotions betrayed her for an unguarded second, as hands fluttered at her throat; but moments later she was controlled again. Douglas leaned forward to touch her cheek, and bravely she returned his reassuring smile; then he joined Holmes and me at the window. Barker and the two policemen stood close by.

As we watched, with a sickening sense of helplessness, the tethered aerostat overtook the train —its anchoring cables taut and straining against the dirigible's velocity. MacDonald and White Mason grasped the situation with admirable dexterity.

"They will try to halt the locomotive in some way," said the CID man. "Once motionless, we shall be helpless!"

"Calm yourself, Mr Mac," cautioned Holmes. "They can do nothing to the engine itself— unless these infernal scowrers are more

deadly than I credit them to be…"

Douglas shook his head. "They might be used to intimidate; but at the range those jaspers must use them—and under the Earth's gravity—it would be a lucky shot indeed to do more than bounce ineffectually off the locomotive."

"And if I were one of the crew," I added, "I should be inclined to open the throttle if someone in an aerostat should begin waving any kind of weapon at me."

As if it had merely awaited my word, the train surged forward, flinging us all temporarily off balance. Holmes' expression was one of wry amusement.

"And now friend Watson adds clairvoyance to his legion of talents."

Douglas had produced the large repeating pistol. He cocked it by means of the trigger-guard lever. "Let me take a crack at them," he growled. "Those pneumatic claws are no match for honest iron!"

"You anticipate my thoughts, Mr Douglas." Holmes glanced up at the carriage's ceiling. "But we will need a much more advantageous spot from which to take pot-shots…"

"You can't mean the roof, Holmes?" I cried.

"Can I not? Where else do you propose? You are the army man, Watson—advise me…"

I had to acknowledge he was correct. But whoever took to the unsteady roof would not only be placing themselves at risk of being thrown to the racing ground below,

but also provide an easy target for the desperate creatures in the stolen aerostat. "And what if they are armed with something more deadly than scowrers?"

But even as Holmes and I stood and debated, Douglas was already at the door. He swung it open, stepped down onto the footboard and—clinging against the horizontal grab irons which lay outside each carriage window—he edged himself towards the carriage-end. In moments he was gone.

MacDonald was all for following him, but Holmes held him back. "It is not for Scotland Yard's finest to go climbing around the roofs of first-class carriages. Nor you, Mr White Mason—nor indeed Mr Barker—" Douglas's friend looked about to protest loudly at that, but Holmes quelled him with a look. "I flatter myself that I retain a certain alacrity which will prove adequate to gaining the roof; whilst Watson here is as sure-footed as a mountain goat—"

I confess that news came as a surprise to me.

"—I cannot allow any of you to risk your lives—"

"Whilst he can apparently risk mine with little regard...," I could not help but interject.

"Ha! Again your bristly humour impales me! Come, Watson—you know you would never forgive me going it alone. Audentes fortuna iuvat!" And with that he too swung himself out of the gaping door and was lost to sight.

White Mason was rubbing his chin. "I have always imagined Mr Holmes to be a stolid, reasoning individual," said he, "but he has quite the impetuous streak."

"Ay—he exists to confound us," said MacDonald with a wry smile. I silently agreed.

"Watch over Mrs Douglas and Barker," said I, quietly. "If the three of us—well, let us say we do not prevail, those men might not be content with just Douglas. I fancy they would silence us all."

MacDonald nodded. "Understood, doctor. Take care yourself, now..."

With understandable trepidation, I approached the open door. It swung gently—propelled by the sway of the moving carriage. Clinging to the window strap with my left hand and the door frame with my right, I felt for the footboard which ran the length of the carriage with the toe of my boot. With both feet firmly on the wide step I released the strap and held onto the frame with both hands then, wishing I was once more the young medical officer who had taken command of a burning aerostat simply because he was too unseasoned to appreciate the risks, I let go with my right hand. Shuffling along the footboard towards the carriage rear, holding dearly onto each set of grab irons at each window I passed—often meeting the startled face of a fellow passenger—I eventually reached the end of the carriage. My right hand closed upon a rail which curved up to the roof. Clinging to it desperately,

I let go of the last grab iron, shuffled the last few inches—with my eyes shut, I believe!—and swung myself flat against the rocking carriage's end.

There were two sets of basic iron steps—four in each—which began above a buffer and met near the apex of the roof. Each set was accompanied by a separate handrail. Should the carriage be stationary, accessing the roof would be simplicity itself; now, it would be a foolhardy—or desperate—individual indeed who attempted it. As two such individuals had preceded me, I could be no less reckless. Holding the rail in both hands, I took the steps carefully, being certain each foot was firmly placed before raising the other. I daresay the ascent took less than a minute; at the time it felt more like a lifetime.

I pulled myself flat onto the roof. Holmes and Douglas had seated themselves comfortably on the raised clerestory; if the American did not hold a raised pistol, they would have been the sedate image of two gentlemen taking a moment of ease. As I pulled myself flat onto the carriage roof, Holmes glanced at me, grinning fiercely.

"Is this not revitalising, Watson? I envy our forebears who rode the rails in open waggons, enjoying the elements!"

I scuttled to his side in the most undignified manner. "Perhaps on that point we may agree to differ," I gasped, sitting myself on the clerestory. I am not ashamed to admit my breathing was as ragged as my heartbeat; I mopped my brow with a handkerchief.

"Stout Watson! Breathe deeply, my dear fellow, for our work is upon us." He indicated the aerostat cable—and the sleek construct which loomed overhead, pacing our train easily. Already it had begun to lower itself down its restraining cables. In the pilot's gondola, positioned amidships on the ventral surface, I could clearly see frantic activity: an access hatch hanging open, an indistinct figure framed within.

"They must wait for the ship to be as low in the air as possible," cried Douglas. The barrel of his huge pistol seemed attached to the dirigible by invisible cords, so steady was his aim. "They cannot hope to strike with any accuracy at a range greater than five yards."

I watched the freighter as its bulk neared inexorably. In those moments I felt some sympathy with the great whales: helpless to flee even as death—in the shape of a black whaling ship—approaches. "So close," I gasped. My breathing was settling at last.

"On the Moon, doctor, a man with a good aim and strong arm could easily manage ten times that distance!"

The sky was eclipsed as the aerostat reached the lowest limit of its tethering cables. Now it seemed to skim the landscape: a leviathan

cruising the ether, our train no more significant to it than a shoal of parasitic fish. The rigid mantle looked close enough to touch. I felt the prickle of tears in my eyes.

"The ammonia employed as buoyancy," explained Holmes, blinking away his own irritation. "Even the most efficient seals may not prevent some trace escaping. At altitude of course it is of no consequence."

I was watching the gondola—now surely within the scowrer's range: through open hatch and the many windows I could clearly see the two putative labourers, now revealed for who they really were as they levelled their strange harpoon weapons.

"The Willabys!" cursed Douglas. He fired his repeater; I heard the shell ricochet off the gondola sides, and had the satisfaction of seeing both men inside shrink aside. "So they escaped the Devil's Bowl shoot-out too!" Outwardly cool, he levered another shell into place and took a second shot—but I perceived the whitened knuckles and bunching jaw muscles. A deep fury possessed the man; God help the Willabys if he took them alive.

This time the occupants of the gondola merely flinched as the bullet failed to hit a significant target. Even as Douglas levered a third shot into the chamber one raised his scowrer and fired. There was a sound somewhere between a sigh and a gulp, and a clawed harpoon struck the edge of the carriage roof. It failed to find purchase, however, and fell away. I heard a distant buzz—with a certain degree of surprise and chagrin, I realised the failed shot was being reeled back.

"You failed to inform us those harpoons were reusable, Mr Douglas!" Holmes was indignant.

"So I did, sir." Douglas fired again. "Consider me admonished."

Glass shattered in the gondola: the second of the Willabys was using the flat butt of his scowrer to smash out the windows. A moment later I heard the pneumatic sob of him firing—but his shot failed to even find the carriage. It rewound quickly.

"What can they hope to gain by hooking us like a salmon?" I cried. "Surely they do not mean to crawl across!"

"If both them scowrers get a good enough hold," growled Douglas, his American accent broadening in the excitement, "they can use 'em as anchors. While one lets out the aerostat's tethers, the other will be rewinding the scowrer's lines…"

"Ha!" Holmes clapped his hands. "They will haul their aerial mount close enough for them to simply leap the gap. They are inventive."

Belatedly a thought occurred to me. "Bridges, Holmes—and tunnels…!"

"Sadly, there are none before London, my dear doctor." He narrowed his eyes. "A detail of which I'm sure our friends are only too aware."

Another scowrer claw impacted upon the roof; this time it sank deep into the wood. There was a savage cry of triumph from the aerostat's gondola, followed by the whir of a rewinding line. And as incredible as it looked to my eyes, it was obvious the vast bulk of the rigid envelope was edging closer to the racing train. Buoyed as it was by ammonia vapour, all visual evidence to the contrary, the aerostat weighed practically nothing. Whilst its electric motors kept it apace of the train, it could be winched between running cable and carriage with no more effort than if it was a toy balloon.

Holmes was upon the straining line in a second. Drawing a knife from his pocket he attempted to cut through the scowrer cable—but fell back with a cry of frustration.

"Toughened aluminum line!" declared Douglas as he took a careful shot at the one holding the scowrer presently embedded in the roof. "Able to withstand the extremes of a lunar day—you're going to need more than just a pocket knife to cut it."

"Evidently!" Holmes was waspish with frustration.

I dodged just in time as the second scowrer fired its toothed harpoon into the edge of the clerestory roof bare inches from where I sat. Clearly, the aerostat was coming into range of those devilish tools. I turned and, seizing the thin line in both hands, I tugged as hard as I might. I was rewarded seconds later as the claws tore free of the wood—almost throwing myself bodily from the roof as it loosened. If Holmes had not floored me with an expert rugby tackle, I shudder to think what may have resulted.

The line ripped free of my grasp; the palms of both hands would certainly have been flayed had I not been wearing thick winter gloves. The clawed end dragged across the roof, ploughing shallow furrows where it passed. Holmes and I came uncertainly to our feet, expecting the rewound line to be fired again directly. Douglas fired again—the hammer of his repeater snapping with a hollow rap on an empty chamber. With admirable cool, the American disconnected the empty magazine and threw it negligently aside, produced a pre-loaded one from his coat, and thrust it into place. He levered a bullet into place and fired—as calmly as if he was competing in a local shooting contest.

The second scowrer was fired again; once more its wicked barbs embedded themselves in the clerestory. I stooped to attempt another extraction, but Holmes' arm upon my shoulder stayed me.

"No, friend Watson—let them come as close as they dare!" By the light in his eyes I knew he had a plan—but it sounded an audacious one.

"If they gain this roof, the outcome will not be at all certain!"

"It will not come to that. Remember the Birlstone railway disaster…" He called out to Douglas: "Can you target the propulsive motors?" He pointed at the electrically-powered impulse motors, contained in plain boxes at the ends of the tethering cables: clamped securely around the running cable. The American smiled with confidence.

"Sir, as a boy I fought Johnny Reb; as a man I have faced down many a redskin. No man alive cannot but attest I hit anything I aim at!"

"Then I would obliged—!"

Douglas lowered the barrel of his repeater, levelling in carefully at the leading drive-box. All the while I watched the colossal aerostat loom ever closer overhead; the hatefully triumphant faces of Douglas's implacable enemies growing clearer with each heartbeat. There was a shot, followed a moment later by another. I dragged my attention away from the aerostat in time to see Douglas fire a third bullet into the motor's housing. The casing buckled and flew apart, exposing the electric impulse drive within.

"Do not miss, Mr Douglas," spoke Holmes.

I divined their intention: if Douglas shot apart the motor, the aerostat would quickly lose impetus—yet still be attached to the train by the scowrer lines. Weightless, it would be dragged in the train's wake faster even than the tethering cables could be paid out. The two men must release their harpoons or risk being snatched from the gondola to an uncertain fate. The American took his fourth shot.

What happened next far exceeded my expectations—although in my darkest moments I often credit Holmes with exactly foreseeing the outcome. As the bullet struck, the lead motor spewed sparks and flames and came to a halt with shocking abruptness. The aerostat wallowed like a baffled whale, its nose dipping sedately as the forward tethering cable ceased all motion. A moment later its tail also dropped, pulled by a motor still running full ahead. The entire dirigible twisted with misleading grace, its weightless bulk towed after the speeding train. But weightless though it may have been, it still had mass, and momentum; the abrupt changes in attitude and velocity drove slow ripples through the rigid mantle as it buckled. The rear motor ran directly into the stalled forward, provoking a further explosion of sparking metal and wiring. Inexorably, the aerostat sank ground-wards.

Even then the vessel may have been saved had the scowrer cables torn themselves free of the carriage roof, or the occupants of the gondola simply ejected their deadly tools. But neither of those events followed. Fate or bigoted determination dictated the proceedings. The aerostat drifted to the ground with a deceptive leisureliness, its mantle heaving as though it was constructed of nothing more inflexible than vulcanized rubber. Dragged after the train, pinned by its tethering cables, the aerostat struck the ground; the impact drove waves up through the crushing mantle. It split.

I saw a lone figure crawl out from under the collapsing frame. He stood uncertainly and took an unsteady step before clutching at his face and throat. Writhing horribly he fell to the ground; after a moment, he moved no more. The ammonia contained in the envelope: deadly when concentrated. I recalled the Birlstone railway disaster: more were killed by the released toxic gas than the crash itself.

The aerostat wreckage spread across the railway line, running cable, and many square yards of farmland beside. There would be no trains to or from London until it was cleared up safely. We managed to lever the embedded scowrer lines free with great effort, coiling them up to recover their considerably battered launchers. MacDonald could add them to his evidence. Back in our compartment Mrs Douglas greeted her husband with tearful relief; Barker shook Holmes and myself by the hand; the two policemen stared at the three of us in mutual disbelief.

"Man," sighed MacDonald as he collapsed back into a seat, "I canna wait to read this adventure!"

AN EVENTFUL EVENING
by Adem Rolfe

As well as novels, we will be recounting the continuing adventures of Holmes and Watson within the Moriarty paradigm through a series of short volumes that alternate between short-story mash-ups based upon the original canon and original stories set very firmly within a steampunk world. Here is an excerpt from our first original short story, The Lavender Men:

It is difficult for a medical man in London to be taken seriously if he does not attend some professional club or society.

While I retain membership of the Abernethians from my student days, it offers little more than an annual dinner and so, over the years I have made a point of guesting at Chandos House every couple of months just to maintain some contact with my fellow professionals. My occasional attendance at the Longchamp—a gift from a grateful patient—notwithstanding, the prospect of parting with a significant amount of money to give me access to a private gentlemen's club, where the drinks are even more expensive, has never appealed.

My first port of call was therefore the surgeon's bar at Saint Barts, where I met with our old friend Stamford. After catching up over a couple of drinks he introduced me to another doctor, Charles Colman, who had heard something of transcendent anatomy as a field of research when, at the Royal Medical and Chirurgical Society, he had heard the thing discussed. He agreed, in return for further drinks, to take me that evening as a guest, and to introduce me to the source of his recollection.

It was a quarter to nine when we arrived at Berners Street, whereupon we were ushered upstairs past the library, the dining room and some meeting rooms, into the lounge. Here Colman called for some cognac before introducing me to Dr. Joshua Pryce of King's College London. He was happy to discuss his understanding of transcendent anatomy with fellow surgeons, for this was the purpose of a professional society after all. Just so long as I kept him well topped up.

"Imagine," Pryce began, "a scientific method by which the human capacity can be improved. Where Francis Galton identified a possible link between ancestry and mental superiority, there have been others who believe that science might be used to make the mind and body more resilient by external means. Just as we use drugs and medical aids to provide relief or to heal, might they not also be used to make the legs faster or the bones stronger or the organs more efficient?"

"That's a reasonable avenue to explore," I agreed, "just so long as the side-effects don't jeopardise the long-term health of the patient. If it puts a man's short-term effectiveness ahead of his long term welfare, then it cannot be allowed."

"Quite, James; although the term patient suggests you are thinking of men with ailments, rather than those deemed fit for military service. In times of war, where the lives of men are bartered for territory and power, such considerations might not be so great."

"So that's what the Knox Institute is about?" I ventured.

Pryce nodded. "Knox poured all his wealth into a research institute in order to apply his expertise in anatomy to the improvement of the body through medicines and appliances. Sir William Fergusson took over when he died, and then Fergusson passed the baton to the current President, Sir Joseph Lister."

"Fergusson and Lister?" I repeated in some surprise. Pryce couldn't have come up with two bigger names in contemporary medicine if he tried.

"Fergusson was pretty hands-on, but for Lister it's mostly titular. A lot of the new electropathic equipment he trials at his new surgical unit comes from the Knox Institute."

I nodded. The aseptic surgery at King's College was reputed to be the best in all of Europe. If I could have my days as a medical student over again it would be my first choice to study there. I resisted questioning Pryce any further for fear of showing too much interest, for it is never a good idea to question the reputation of a surgeon as great as Lister. I changed the topic to more pleasurable pursuits like golf and fly-fishing, making my excuses as the evening drew to a close and returning to Baker Street at the first opportunity.

It was close to midnight when I returned to our rooms, and the streets were quite deserted. In the distance I spied a faint glow and a thin pall of smoke to the south of the river—a warehouse or slum fire I presumed. The older parts of the city were overcrowded and in need of much rebuilding. As my cab pulled up outside our Baker Street rooms I could see Holmes' brilliantly lit silhouette as he paced back and forth, pausing only to acknowledge my arrival through the window.

With the hour being late Holmes came down to greet me, and, I am sure, to check my sobriety. It had been a long night for me, and I could already smell the spirit through my pores. Unusually, he sat me down and waited upon my own experiences before launching into an account of his own.

"Splendid work, Watson. I agree that, with Lister and Fergusson behind it, the Knox Institute has impeccable credentials. There is more

to this matter than meets the eye, which is why I took a little excursion down to the offices of the Medical Ordnance Company in Southwark for a spot of breaking and entering earlier this evening."

"You did what?" I was quite angry with Holmes, sending me off to get tipsy while he was risking his reputation on an undeniably criminal act.

"You should know by now Watson, that I do not do these things without careful consideration. I first disguised myself as a dragon-chaser out of Limehouse. The heavy stink of opium smoke and my apparent lethargy would buy me the time I might need to make my escape and to not be taken seriously if discovered; a precaution it was well for me to take."

"The Ordnance Company lies off the Jamaica Road not far past Shad Thames. A rough spot in the daytime, it looks even worse at night. I couldn't have got closer to the docks without being in Bermondsey itself, and I suspect the location was chosen precisely because of its easy access to the river. It has high walls and no accessible windows, with the only point of entry being a guarded arch. Fortunately, the south-facing wall was in a poor state of repair, and a tree brushed across the top at the midpoint between a pair of old gas street lamps not yet upgraded. Even better, the wood was sturdy enough for me to cast a rope over its bough and pulley myself up using a looped knot. From there I could see the bough continued some feet past the wall, over an enclosed courtyard."

"Balancing upon the wall, I counted three storeys altogether, with barred windows on the first two. The only way up to that level was a cast iron drainpipe, which I decided to risk. Dropping to the ground I produced the leather climbing strap—the one we recovered from the Tudor Mansions case—and tested the pipe against my weight. It was then a matter of a minute or two to pull myself up to the higher level, where a wide ledge allowed me to use my bradawl to attack the heavy sash mechanism with some vigour."

"I confess I was uncertain of what my evening's investigations might reveal, but every room presents a different opportunity. The top floor was clearly administrative, and I was able to view a number of patent records for devices trialled and tested by the Knox Institute and then manufactured by the Ordnance Company. Most of these apparati related to the manufacture of body braces, harnesses, clevis pins and armoured casings to protect the various electropathic stimulators or chemical injectors. There were miniaturized timing mechanisms, and all manner of prostheses and implantations. All perfectly legitimate from a medical perspective, but quite suspicious in combination."

"Dissatisfied with mere paperwork, I descended lower, into what I assumed was the manufactory. The first floor was a high-ceilinged, open space, and in the moonlight that flooded through the windows I could make out assembly tables and parts baskets, lasts and lathes and material swatches. All the things one might expect in a workshop producing medical harnesses. But there was more."

"The workshop was lined with incandescent bulbs, and I was able to fill the room with brilliant light as I flicked on a switch close to the door. Where there had been shadows I could now see that around a dozen cages lined the inner wall of the workshop. Each of these contained a strap-down tilt-table on which—"

"Yes, Holmes," I encouraged him, "what did you see?"

"They were men, Watson, strapped to the tables and sleeping like the dead. Beside each was a neat pile of clothes—their East India uniforms. They wore only undergarments beneath elasticated body braces, and each man was connected to a number of intravenous catheters. You would have made more of it than I, but to a layman's eye these tubes appeared to be drawing thick black blood out of their bodies, passing it through a spinning mechanism that distilled it into a bright red form, and then mixing it with fluid from another catheter before returning it back into their bodies."

"Filtering poisons from the blood I presume. Did you sample the additive?"

"I did," said he, drawing a small brown bottle from his pocket. He passed the drug to me and I unscrewed the lid, withdrawing the small glass pipette. I sniffed the concoction. It was a saline tincture that included morphine, aconite and something akin to celery or fennel.

"A potent anaesthetic," I concluded, urging Holmes to continue.

"Fortunately for me. I suspect the poisons being filtered were created by infections."

"Why do you say that, Holmes?"

"Each man appeared to have various body parts tied off to eliminate the flow of blood. As Murray had observed, there was an overwhelming smell of lavender oil, but beneath it I could smell the rot. Arms and legs were isolated by metal pins inserted through flesh and bone, then capped with rubber seals liberally applied with alcohol and iodine as if to stave off the spread of their infection."

"That's appalling, Holmes. Surely the army cannot be complicit in that?"

"Not the army, Watson, but the New East India Company. I am not a religious man, but the application of the science of transcendent anatomy can only be described as unholy."

"Indeed," said I, as shocked as my companion. I thought back to Pryce's description of the work, and shuddered at the thought of someone doing this in a time of relative peace. "What happened next?"

"I made an error of judgement, Watson. One so terrible that I will be forced to live with the consequences until my final breath. The cages, you see, were only locked from the inside, and I was desperate to make a further inspection. Opening the nearest, I stepped inside and examined the man that lay there more closely."

"There were no personal effects or papers identifying him, but there was, tied to his neck with butcher's twine, a Prussian hundemark."

"A what?"

"A dog tag. Used on the streets of Berlin to mark the ownership of dogs, the Prussian army adopted them as a means of identifying the injured and the dead during the Franco-Prussian War. Several armies have considered using them, and I must assume the New East Indias have adopted the practice. This one was round and made of soft brown metal, into which some basic information— the letters NEIC followed by name, rank, service number and a date— had been crudely impressed. His name was Ashleigh, and he had been a Corporal. The date intrigued me— 04-08-79—not a date of birth, for he would be only five years old, so what? The date he joined the Grey Company, perhaps?"

"Up close I withdrew my pocket knife and cut away his vest to examine him in more detail. He was hairless, and his chest was marred by multiple scars which, from their length and the quality of the stitches, must have been medical in nature."

"Finally, and most foolishly, I withdrew the catheters, holding back the last—the one pushing bright red blood into his veins— until the very last moment. Optimistically I had brought a small vial of smelling salts with me, which I applied before standing well back, for I desperately wanted to speak with the man. At first there was no reaction, so I waited a few moments before applying the salts again, and this time he reacted. It was a deep, guttural moan, soon followed by the flickering of his eyelids and the clarity of consciousness within his pupils. He stared at me, Watson, his bloodshot eyes conveyed not just the depth of his pain, but also the anger and distress that his condition had instilled upon him. Within moments he was straining hard against the leather straps of the tilt-table, and I considered, very briefly, releasing him from his bondage. There was, however, no need, for the straining of his muscles against the leather soon caused it to snap. I stood there, my voice hoarse, questions racing through my mind. His eyes fixed upon me as I stepped back, out of the cage. The pupils were wide, and there was no sign of any muscular activity in the face, which remained impassive even as the body strained to unleash itself."

"Uncertain of what to expect, I tried to reason with Corporal

Ashleigh; to calm him down. Eventually, detached from the tilt-table, he took a step towards me and spoke at last."

"'Halt,' he said in a raw and stilted voice, 'Identify yourself!'"

"Naturally, I backed away as he stretched his hands out towards me, but I found my retreat blocked by worktables. I delivered a flurry of neat blows to his nose, jaw and abdomen, but it was like punching a side of beef. He easily swatted my fists aside before his hands quickly and precisely found my windpipe. I have never been in greater fear for my life than at that moment, when the image of my death at the hands of some inhuman beast flashed before my eyes. I was leaning so far backwards that I feared my spine might give before I lost consciousness, while this... creature that so resembled Mary Shelley's creation bore down upon me."

"I desperately scrabbled for a makeshift weapon on the worktable behind me. Even as pins and needles closed around my head I could feel the haft of something loose within my grasp. Swinging it around with all the force that I could muster, I found myself plunging a screwdriver deep into the side of my attacker's head, perforating the eardrum and driving it directly into the left hand side of his brain."

"The Corporal's fingers opened involuntarily and I gasped for breath. A moment later I saw a trickle of blood emerge from one of his nostrils. I jiggled my makeshift weapon as he pressed upon me again, sliding myself from beneath his heavy body as he crashed onto the work-top."

"Gasping for air, I resolved to brush up on my hand-to-hand skills, for my survival had been due more to chance than to preparation. Even then, with his brains scrambled, the Corporal lurched up with a manic glint in his eye, and reached again for me. I placed my foot squarely onto his midsection and pushed, tipping him to the floor where, again, he began to stir. A glance to the worktable revealed an toolbox, which I took a hold of, heaving it solidly above my head before using all my remaining strength to hurl it directly onto his head."

"Good grief, Holmes," I said at last, having found myself wince at the graphic nature of my friend's account. As a doctor I had seen and heard a great many things, but this was unlike any I had heard, and to see fear in Holmes' recollections was a new experience for me, for nothing had shaken him as deeply as this encounter with the lavender men. "What happened next? The others—".

"So help me, Watson, I made sure that he was dead, and then I gathered up the hundemarken from the others while they slept and then... I killed them. I killed them all. I smashed the fluid bottles and spread alcohol

across the workshop. I ignited a match and then retreated to the top floor where I set fire to all the records I had found there before making my escape. Even as we speak the factory burns."

THE SCIENCE OF DEDUCTION
by Damon Cavalchini

In a few short years the mash-up has already earned a reputation as something that juxtaposes classic fiction with elements of comedy and horror, but with Sherlock Holmes we are taking mystery fiction and superimposing the steampunk aesthetic. Doyle's stories were precursors to the later pulp adventures, and so its adaptation as a series of fast-paced adventure thrillers takes little from the original. Here, in an excerpt from Damon Cavalchini's Sign of V, we can see how little often needs to be added to the original to create the kind of story that we want to tell:

It was a September afternoon and this Tuesday had been a dreary one, a dense drizzly fog lay low upon the great city. A satin covering rose from the River Thames, knotted with steam from the many factories on the city's outskirts and draped London in mist like the public rooms in a giant Turkish bath. From the window, I watched a parade of mechanical carriages cough their way along the tar-cut surface of Baker Street, an unmistakable stutter as they slowed for the urchins who ran blindly across the street. Horses brayed at having to share their roads with these strange new beasts and a hansom cab jerked as a fume of noxious smoke belched from a mechanical carriage, adding to the groggy haze. The powerful fans of the overhead aerostats groaned and swung amongst the buildings on their cables. We live in a world of wonders and changes that leave this poor child of Scotland amazed. No longer for me the highland beauty and simplicity of my childhood. A pale moon hung in the afternoon sky, a faint circle glowing like a spotlight behind the curtain of fog, watching our sprawling metropolis, our mother city, below. To think, only months ago, my dear friend Sherlock Holmes had walked on the surface of our nearest celestial body, chasing a horror of death.

Compared to which the wonderful advances of modern London dimmed, dulled but not diminished by her cloak of fog and steam. London was no quiet country town where you could lie in the sweet embrace of silence. The crow-like call of progress always squawked, destroying any hope of a tranquil afternoon. There was an underlying growl of people from the street below, the shrill of the beggars and the shouts of young boys hawking the evening papers swallowed up by the din of the modern city.

Not that Holmes cared in the slightest. To him, advances such as these just happened. He found no value in wondering about the impact of such devices on our way of life, no point in embracing the thrill of change, except insofar as they related to his own curious profession. As I have mentioned in previous works, he focused his attention on his own private interests and chose not to clutter his mind with the same things which consumed you or I.

Ignoring the outside world, Holmes rose from the comfort of the chaise longue, moved towards the corner of the mantelpiece and retrieved his latest purchase from William Gulliver and Sons. With his long, white, nervous fingers he adjusted the delicate needle and rolled back his left shirt cuff. But he did not have a toothache nor did his slender frame have a need to diet—these being the more common triggers for this particular treatment. Holmes' condition was different. His thin frame, already overworked, stretched in an explosion of energy. Then stopped. For some little time his eyes rested thoughtfully upon the sinewy forearm and wrist, all dotted and scarred with innumerable puncture-marks. Finally, he thrust the sharp point home, pressed down the tiny piston, and sank back into the velvet-lined armchair with a long sigh of satisfaction.

Three times a day I had observed Holmes' performance, less often than many of London's writers and artists, but far more often than a retired army officer could afford. Despite the growing familiarity, I refused to become accustomed to the practice. I had, from day to day, become more irritable at the sight as my conscience weighed nightly upon me at the thought that I might lack the courage to protest. I have long followed the teachings of Dr Thomas Allinson, and yet the weight of opinion held by most of my fellow practitioners stifled my protests before they could rise. Again and again I had registered a vow that I should deliver my soul upon the subject, but there was something in the cool, nonchalant air of my companion which made him the last man with whom one would care to take anything approaching to a liberty. The last few times I had raised my concerns, during that Birlstone business and in our adventure with that Bohemian scoundrel, I had been proven wrong. Despite my concerns, his skills proved greater than any handicap the drugs might have provided. His great powers, his masterly manner, and the experience which I had had of his many extraordinary qualities, all made me diffident and backward in confronting him.

Yet upon that afternoon, whether it was the Beaune which I had taken with my lunch, or the additional exasperation produced by the extreme deliberation of his manner, I suddenly felt that I could hold out no longer.

"Which is it today?" I asked, forcing myself to resume my seat. "Morphine or cocaine?"

He raised his eyes languidly from the old black-letter volume which he had opened. "It is cocaine—" he said, "—a seven-per-cent solution. Would you care to try it?"

"No, indeed," I answered, brusquely. "As you know my constitution has not yet fully recovered from my Afghan campaign. I cannot afford to throw any extra strain upon it."

I had served the British and Indian Troops during the Second Afghan War, providing medical aid where I could, until I was eventually assigned as Surgeon-Lieutenant to the Berkshires. My sense of duty to the crown and the great heart of the British people grew beyond measure during those years. It was one of the proudest times of my life before I met Holmes. It was during my service aboard the relief airship Keane during the Battle of Maiwand in the year 1880, that I sustained the injuries destined to plague me for the rest of my life. Downed by enemy rockets, the Keane crashed in mountains over the Panjshir Valley, and as senior surviving officer I was responsible for leading the survivors back to Kabul. Those days were some of the roughest of my life. My pale skin felt forever burned by the sun which were so unlike the mild caress of the English summer. Like many of our party, my skin also carried the memory of the flames which had consumed our craft as we fell from the sky. Our party of wounded trekked through the wild plants and trees avoiding insects and snipers alike, each with the same deadly earnest. By the time we reached the camp, I had formed friendships which I have never abandoned. Even during my time with Holmes I made a point of visiting The Longchamp on the last Friday of the month whenever funds allowed. While my injuries were not extensive—some shrapnel was embedded in different parts of the left-hand side of my body, which also suffered minor burns—they did leave me prone to an enteric fever that nearly killed me and which succeeded in ending my military career.

To address my injuries, I was treated with a local concoction of powdered cannabis leaves, mixed with sugar and fried in ghee with black pepper and poppy seeds, which possibly explained my vehemence at Holmes' casual use of such substances. While current medical practice saw no problem with such behaviour, it was an experience I would not readily repeat. Nor were effects ones which I would wish on my dear friend.

Holmes smiled at the strength of my vehemence. "Perhaps you are right, Watson," he said. "I suppose that its influence is physically a bad one. I find it, however, so

transcendently stimulating and clarifying to the mind that its secondary action is a matter of small moment."

"But consider!" I said, earnestly. "Count the cost! Your brain may, as you say, be roused and excited, but it is a pathological and morbid process, which involves increased tissue-change and may, at the last, leave a permanent weakness. You know, too, what a black reaction comes upon you when the effects diminish. Surely the game is hardly worth the candle if you burn up all your energy? Why should you, for a mere passing pleasure, risk the loss of those great powers with which you have been endowed? Remember that I speak not only as one comrade to another, but as a medical man to one for whose constitution he is to be held, to some extent, answerable."

Holmes did not seem offended. On the contrary, he put his finger-tips together and leaned his elbows on the arms of his favourite wicker chair, like one who has a relish for the conversation. It was another distraction. A beggar's choice but one he still accepted gratefully.

"My mind—" he said, "—rebels at stagnation. Give me problems, give me work, give me the most abstruse cryptogram or the most intricate analysis, and I am in my own proper atmosphere. I can dispense then with artificial stimulants. But I abhor the dull routine of existence. I crave for mental exaltation. We've had

this discussion before and you have never been able to convince me of the logic of your arguments. Even the Viennese doctor Freud extols its virtues in curing the monomania of boredom. And that is the mixture's prime gift. I know your concerns but you are still in the minority of learned opinion. Do not think I do not value your advice and consternation, my friend. If I could only find such distractions in ongoing work I would have no need to visit Lower Belgrave Street. As you well know, that is why I have chosen my own particular profession—or rather created it, for I am the only one in the world."

"The only unofficial detective?" I said, raising my eyebrows, having heard this conceit previously. My companion was a dear friend but occasionally his need for engagement with a challenge overcame his manners. He needed the confrontation, seeking a foe against which to test his mettle. Even something so simple as debating with me about his work. For all his claims of being the only one, a quick glance at his desk could inform even an inexperienced observer such as myself of the lie of his assertion. Indeed his desk was covered in letters from other private detectives whose calls for his advice he responded to from the comfort of our parlour.

"The only unofficial consulting detective," he answered, repeating his often held summary of his role. Nitpicking. I had never completely agreed with the fancies of the distinction. "I am the last and highest court of appeal in detection. When Gregson or Lestrade or even Athelney Jones are out of their depths— which, by the way, is their normal state—the matter is laid before me. I examine the data, as an expert, and pronounce a specialist's opinion. I claim no credit in such cases. My name figures in no newspaper. The work itself, the pleasure of finding a field for my peculiar powers, is my highest reward. But you have yourself had some experience of my methods of work in the Jefferson Hope case."

"Yes, indeed," said I, cordially. "I was never so struck by anything in my life, having embodied it in a small brochure entitled 'The Lauriston Gardens Mystery'."

He shook his head sadly. "I glanced over it," said he. "Honestly, I cannot congratulate you upon it. As we have often discussed, detection is, or ought to be, an exact science, and should be treated in the same cold and unemotional manner. You have attempted to tinge it with romanticism, which produces much the same effect as if you worked a love-story or an elopement into the fifth proposition of Euclid."

"But the romance was there," I remonstrated. "Especially in my own case. I could not tamper with the facts."

"Some facts should be suppressed, or at least a just sense of proportion should be observed in treating them.

The only point in the case which deserved mention was the curious analytical reasoning from effects to causes by which I succeeded in unravelling it."

I was annoyed at this criticism of a work which had been specially designed to please him. I confess, too, that I was irritated by the egotism which seemed to demand that every line of my pamphlet should be devoted to his special doings. Indeed I had argued with a fellow writer, whose generosity in helping prepare my diaries for publication saw many more changes in emphasis than I had intended. I should be clear while I keep these diaries in the hope of publishing more of my friend's adventures, my own practice, Holmes' continuing adventures and my lack of contacts within the publishing industry meant that I intended to leave the act of editing and preparing these words for eventual publication to my friend and colleague, Dr. Arthur Conan Doyle.

It was an arrangement which suited us both. While Conan Doyle is a writer with more than a few works written entirely by him successfully published, he does suffer from the weakness of never having actually lived with Sherlock Holmes. Or the blessing as I sometimes call it. More than once during the years that I had shared rooms with Holmes in Baker Street I had observed that no small vanity underlay my companion's quiet and didactic manner. I made no remark about his criticisms, however, but sat nursing my wounded pride. For all his dismissal of my writings, these very accounts were responsible for introducing him to many of his more unusual cases, helping to advance his burgeoning career. It was a matter of pride that even though he sought no credit for his work, the authorities would only acknowledge their failings so often and, had he relied on Scotland Yard alone for business, we would have found ourselves seeking more affordable lodgings well before now.

For all our advances, one of the most appreciated inventions in recent times was that of the mechanical footrest. My injured leg did not prevent me from walking but still ached wearily at every change of the weather. Thus, as I leant back into the sturdy wooden frame of my chair, I was able to adjust the height of footstool simply by turning a lever of the side. Gears clicked with cogs and the beige pillow rose to meet my foot.

"My practice has extended recently to the Continent," said Holmes after a while, reaching for his old brier-root pipe. "I was consulted last week by Francois Le Villard, who, as you probably know, has come rather to the front lately in the French detective service. He has all the

Celtic power of quick intuition, but he is deficient in the wide range of exact knowledge which is essential to the higher developments of his art. You have seen the value of my own notebooks. Should a fire ever claim this room, or Mrs Hudson be possessed by the unavoidable desire to clean, the science of deduction would be set back decades. Take the matter Le Villard referred to me. The case was concerned with a will, and possessed some features of interest. I was able to refer him to two parallel cases, the one at Riga in 1857, and the other at St. Louis in 1871, which have suggested to him the true solution. Here is the letter which I had this morning acknowledging my assistance."

He tossed over, as he spoke, a crumpled sheet of foreign notepaper. In a sign of the respect that Le Villard held for my friend, he had dispensed with the current practice of sending acknowledgements via the electrograph system and returned to the time-honoured practice of posting a letter. Should it ever become less expensive to send a teslegram than to write a heartfelt message on paper, the Post Office would be at dire risk. Yet as long as lovers and poets need words to share their thoughts and feelings, the letter will survive. Indeed it would be sad day if ever the strength of our hearts was constrained to the brevity imposed by wireless communication.

I glanced my eyes down it, catching

a profusion of notes of admiration, with stray "magnifiques," "coup-de-maitres," and "tours-de-force," all testifying to the ardent admiration of the Frenchman.

"He speaks as a pupil to his master," said I.

"Oh, he rates my assistance too highly," said Sherlock Holmes, lightly, reaching for a packet of his favourite black shag. "He has considerable gifts himself. He possesses two out of the three qualities necessary for the ideal detective. He has the power of observation and that of deduction. He is only wanting in knowledge; and that may come in time. He is now translating my small works into French."

"Your works?" For a moment I thought Holmes had been preparing his own descriptions of his cases and feared Conan Doyle's reaction. I almost laughed at the thought of how much editing Doyle would have to do to make those tomes palatable to his friends in Fleet Street. After his latest critique of my own efforts, the concept was one I almost wished were true.

"Oh, didn't you know?" he cried, laughing. "Yes, I have been guilty of several monographs. They are all upon technical subjects. Here, for example, is one 'Upon the Distinction between the Ashes of the Various Tobaccoes'. In it I enumerate a hundred and forty forms of cigar-, cigarette-, and pipe-tobacco, with coloured plates illustrating the

difference in the ash. It is a point which is continually turning up in criminal trials, and which is sometimes of supreme importance as a clue. If you can say definitely, for example, that some murder has been done by a man who was smoking an Indian lunkah, it obviously narrows your field of search. To the trained eye there is as much difference between the black ash of a Trichinopoly and the white fluff of bird's-eye as there is between a cabbage and a potato."

He chose to emphasise his point by tapping his own discarded ashes on the arm of the chair.

"You have an extraordinary genius for minutiae," I remarked, politely refraining from mentioning how such extraordinary genius sometimes required extraordinary patience to live with.

"I appreciate their importance. Here—" Holmes stopped and pulled a thin pamphlet from the bookshelf, "—is my monograph upon the tracing of footsteps, with some remarks upon the uses of plaster of Paris as a preserver of impresses. Here, too, is a curious little work upon the influence of a trade upon the form of the hand, with lithotypes of the hands of slaters, sailors, corkcutters, compositors, weavers, and diamond-polishers and even the maligned electrograph operators with the unique impression regular use of the device leaves on their fingers. As for the men who dangle from the heavens to repair the cables stretched above our city, the black tar beneath their nails makes it impossible for them to branded with any other occupation. These studies are a matter of great practical interest to the scientific detective—especially in cases of unclaimed bodies—or in discovering the antecedents of criminals. As science expands our world, so too should it expand the largesse of our criminals, and how we catch them. But I weary you with my hobby."

"Not at all," I answered, earnestly, glad for any chance to continue the discussion which paralleled my earlier musing on the new London of this age of steam. "It is of the greatest interest to me, especially since I have had the opportunity of observing your practical application of it. But you spoke just now of observation and deduction. Surely the one, to some extent, implies the other."

"Why, hardly," he answered, leaning back luxuriously in his arm-chair, and sending up thick blue wreaths from his pipe. "For example, observation shows me that you have been to the Wigmore Street Post Office this morning, but deduction lets me know that when there you dispatched a telegram."

"Right!" said I. "Right on both points! But I confess that I don't see how you arrived at it. It was a sudden impulse upon my part, and I have mentioned it to no one."

"It is simplicity itself," he remarked, chuckling at my surprise, "—so absurdly simple that an explanation is superfluous; and yet it may serve to define the limits of observation and of deduction. Observation tells me that you have a little reddish mould adhering to your instep. Just opposite the Seymour Street Office they have taken up the pavement while they make the surface more appropriate for mechanical carriages and thrown up some earth which lies in such a way that it is difficult to avoid treading in it upon entering. At this point you would have found the office closed and a sign advising you to proceed to the nearest office in Wigmore Street. Soil with this peculiar reddish tint is found, as far as I know, nowhere else in the neighborhood. So much is observation. The rest is deduction."

"How, then, did you deduce the telegram?"

"Why, of course, I knew that you had not written a letter, since I sat opposite to you all morning. I see also in your open desk there that you had already recently purchased a sheet of stamps and a thick bundle of post-cards. What could you go into the post-office for, then, but to send a telegram?"

Holmes would have known the Wigmore Street office had yet to install one of the new Teslagraph machines, relying instead on the proven, and less expensive, methods of the telegram. It had been become a mark of status to have a personal Teslagraph along with the accursed intrusion of a telephone located in your own home. While most of my patients could not afford either device when I had my practice with Stamford, those who could made an distinct point of telephoning for an appointment. I found my eyes drawn to the small machine Holmes had badgered Mrs Hudson into having installed during that business with the King of Bohemia earlier in the year. Typically Holmes had failed to consult me and I returned from a busy few days away with my practice to find the mass of wires hanging from the wall. Given Holmes' extensive use of telegrams, his decision to purchase a Teslagraph made sense. Mrs Hudson had installed a telephone a few years earlier as Holmes' business began to blossom. Holmes had compromised in that instance and at least the telephone was located in the parlour rather than our sitting room.

"By the way—" Sherlock continued, "—you have no reason to be concerned about using the machine here. The one in our rooms is working perfectly so your message must have contained material you did not wish me to read or which you felt was inappropriate for discussion on a shared machine."

It still astounded me as to how simple Holmes' explanations sounded when he led me through his reasoning. Indeed, it was his ability to observe my failure to write a letter which had led me to send my missive from the public but, by value of being away from Baker Street, relatively private desks of the Post Office. I mentioned as much to him, causing him to smile in amusement.

"Touche, Watson. As you experienced, I cannot help but observe my surroundings which led to my unintentional intrusion into your privacy. Especially when there is little else to occupy my attention. As for the telegram instead of the teslegram, when you eliminate all other factors, the one which remains must be the truth," he replied.

"In this case it certainly is so," I replied, after a little thought. "The case of my visit to the Post Office is, however, as you say, a matter of the simplest consideration. Would you think me impertinent if I were to put your theories to a more severe test?"

"On the contrary—" he answered, "—it would prevent me from taking a second dose of cocaine. I should be delighted to look into any problem which you might submit to me."

Sensing an opportunity to at least delay the use of another dose of his cocaine mixture, I produced a pocket watch from my jacket and unclipped the chain.

"I have heard you say that it is difficult for a man to have any object in daily use without leaving the impress of his individuality upon it in such a way that a trained observer might read it. Now, I have here a watch which has recently come into my possession. Would you have the kindness to let me have an opinion upon the character or habits of the late owner?"

I handed him over the watch with some slight feeling of amusement in my heart, for the test was, as I thought, an impossible one, and I intended it as a lesson against the somewhat dogmatic tone which he occasionally assumed. Regularly assumed, if the truth be told. The watch featured a mechanical movement, elegant arrows slowly rotating around the intricate backing, and though bruised by time and used, there were delicate engraved designs on the hunter case and the back. He balanced the watch in his hand, gazed hard at the dial, opened the back, and examined the works, first with his naked eyes and then with a powerful convex lens. A smile passed my lips as his fingers pried open the lid to observe the open 'skeleton' dial which allowed the wearer to see the intricate mechanical movement within, indeed I often opened the watch not to determine how many hours had passed by, but to marvel at the skill devoted to so simple an act as telling the time, and I could hardly keep from smiling at his crestfallen face when he finally snapped the case to and handed it back.

"There are hardly any data," he remarked, a distinct look of displeasure on his face. Pouted lines which I had rarely seen creased his lips and forehead. "The watch has been recently cleaned, which robs me of my most suggestive facts."

"You are right," I answered. "It was cleaned before being sent to me." In my heart I accused my companion of putting forward a most lame and impotent excuse to cover his failure. What extra data could he expect from an uncleaned watch? A deduction as to the amount of lint accumulated in a pocket?

"Though unsatisfactory, my research has not been entirely barren," he observed, staring up at the ceiling with dreamy, lack-lustre eyes. "Subject to your correction, I should judge that the watch belonged to your elder brother, who inherited it from your father."

"That you gather, no doubt, from the H. W. upon the back?" It was a simple deduction and one which hardly justified the assuredness of his earlier claims.

"Quite so. The W. suggests your own name. The date of the watch is nearly fifty years back, and the initials are as old as the watch, so it was clearly made for the last generation. It is evidently a man's watch so the rational deduction is that it belonged to your father. Such jewellery usually descends to the eldest son, and he is most likely to have the same name as the father. Your father has, if I remember right, been dead many years. It has, therefore, been in the hands of your eldest brother."

"Right, so far," said I, still unimpressed. "Anything else?"

"He was a man of untidy habits—very untidy and careless. He was left with good prospects, but he threw away his chances, lived for some time in poverty with occasional short intervals of prosperity, and finally, taking to drink, he died. That is all I can gather."

I sprang from my chair and limped impatiently about the room with considerable bitterness in my heart. "This is unworthy of you, Holmes," I said, stung after his earlier blunt dismissal of my concerns about his possible invasion of my personal affairs. "I could not have believed that you would have descended to this. You have made inquiries into the history of my unhappy brother without consulting me, and you now pretend to deduce this knowledge in some fanciful way. You cannot expect me to believe that you have read all this from his old watch! It is unkind and, to speak plainly, has a touch of charlatanism in it."

"My dear doctor—" said he, kindly raising a hand and indicating for me to resume my chair, "— pray accept my apologies. Viewing the matter as an abstract problem, I had forgotten how personal and painful a thing it might be to you. I assure you, however, that I never even knew that you had a brother until you handed me the watch."

"Then how in the name of all that is wonderful did you get these facts? They are absolutely correct in every particular."

"Ah, that is good luck. I could only say what was the balance of

probability. I did not at all expect to be so accurate."

"But it was not mere guess-work?" I was disappoint at the idea he had simply plucked my brother's unfortunate history from the air.

"No, no, Watson, I never guess. It is a shocking habit—destructive to the logical faculty. Deduction moves from general truths, such as the common act of a father passing an heirloom to his eldest son, to the specific, such as the initial on the plate. What seems strange to you is only so because you do not follow my train of thought or observe the small facts upon which large inferences may depend. For example, I began by stating that your brother was careless. When you observe the lower part of that watch-case you notice that it is not only dinted in two places, but it is cut and marked all over from the habit of keeping other hard objects, such as coins or keys, in the same pocket. Surely it is no great feat to assume that a man who treats a fifty-guinea watch so cavalierly must be a careless man. Neither is it a very far-fetched inference that a man who inherits one article of such value is pretty well provided for in other respects."

I nodded, to show that I followed his reasoning. Although privately I had some doubts. Many of my patients often possessed only one such precious heirloom amongst a miasma of debt and challenge, one such gift they prized above all others.

And yet, in this case as in so many others, Holmes had arrived at the correct conclusion.

"It is very customary for pawnbrokers in England—" Holmes continued, "—when they take a watch, to scratch the number of the ticket with a pin-point upon the inside of the case. It is more handy than a label, as there is no risk of the number being lost or transposed. There are no less than four such numbers visible to my lens on the inside of this case. Inference—that your brother was often at low water. Secondary inference—that he had occasional bursts of prosperity, or he could not have redeemed the pledge. Finally, I ask you to look at the inner plate, which contains the key-hole. Look at the thousands of scratches all around the hole—marks where the key has slipped. What sober man's key could have scored those grooves? Only one with a medical condition. But you will never see a drunkard's watch without them. So again I chose the most likely one with the alternative as my second option. He winds it at night, and he leaves these traces of his unsteady hand. Where is the mystery in all this?"

"It is as clear as daylight," I answered, admitting to myself that his deductions were accurate. "I regret the injustice which I did you. I should have had more faith in your marvellous faculty. May I ask whether you have any professional inquiry on foot at present?"

Although, sadly I knew the answer. Nothing had attracted his attention in the past few months. Given his moods of late, even his brother Mycroft had been unwilling to refer clients to him. I did not know what had come between the two men but I feared the pervasive influence of Moriarty, given Mycroft's role in the government. It would not surprise me for country and career to come between the two brothers, especially as Moriarty's star was rising in the parliamentary ranks.

"None," Holmes confirmed sadly. "Hence the cocaine. I cannot live without brain-work. What else is there to live for? I stand at the window here and see nothing."

It was the same window at which I had stood earlier and admired the wonders of our new world. But the interest I beheld had no joy for my companion.

"Was it ever such a dreary, dismal, unprofitable world? See how the grey fog swirls down the street and drifts across the dun-coloured houses. What could be more hopelessly prosaic and material? You talk about your new machines and the wonders of the modern age but what good do they do me? What is the use of having powers, doctor, when one has no field upon which to exert them? Crime is commonplace, existence is commonplace, and no qualities save those which are commonplace have any function upon earth."

My eyes lingered on a copy of the Times from a few days previously, still draped across the arm of a chair. "And what about this ghastly murder in Buck's Row?" I said, referring to the brutal death of a prostitute a week earlier.

"That is the providence of Scotland Yard and if they have need of my help, and they indubitably will, they know where to find me." My annoyance at his cold dismissal of such a vicious and inhuman crime must have shown for my companion continued his argument. "Petty murders are no more interesting to me than a husband's lurid affair with his wife's parlour maid. There may be public outcry but where is the mystery apart from the identity of the murderer? What challenge is there except in unmasking his identity? I have every faith even the most uninspired servant of Scotland Yard has as much chance of catching a killer as I. Murderers in Whitechapel are as common pickpockets in East End. The police will knock on doors and question her associates and eventually they will find an embittered client, a spurned partner or particularly puritanical family member who objected to her profession. Would you have me chasing every unsolved slaughter on our gaslit streets? Besides, with a sobriquet like Leather Apron, our killer will never capture the imagination of Fleet Street. No, Watson, unless the killer continues to commit such crimes the press will move on to another tragedy and we will all, sadly, have forgotten the cause of so much recent fervour."

I had not heard the murderer referred to as Leather Apron for the Star would not run their article labelling the killer as such until the next morning. So, despite his intended dismissal, Holmes had taken an interest in the killing and probably enjoyed a private conversation with Scotland Yard. For all his protestations of devotion to logic alone, my companion had a deep sense of justice which often expressed itself in his commitment to his cases. I opened my mouth to reply to this tirade, when with a crisp knock our landlady entered, bearing a card upon the brass salver. Having ceased to employ the services of Mrs Turner in June, Mrs Hudson now oversaw the running of the household

personally. The page-boy, Billy, must have been elsewhere engaged or granted a day off. A small card which it would become clear came straight from providence for both of us.

"A young lady for you, sir," she said, addressing my companion.

"Miss Mary Morstan," he read. "Hum! I have no recollection of the name. Ask the young lady to step up, Mrs Hudson." I started to rise to absent myself to my room when Holmes waved for me to sit. "Don't go, doctor. I should prefer that you remain."

With those words, hope that the card carried a case to inspire my friend's desperate quest for a challenge sprung exultant on triumphant wing.

Little did I know I would be the one to gain the greatest treasure as a result of the case.

SOME PERSONALIA ABOUT MYSELF AND MR. SHERLOCK HOLMES

John Watson must have placed complete trust in his editor and fellow professional, Conan Doyle, but just as his co-editor occasionally felt the need to set the record straight, so too did the other good doctor:

At the request of the publisher, I have spent some days sifting through the old letter box in which, from time to time, letters relating directly or indirectly to my good friend Mr. Sherlock Holmes, courtesy of the Strand Magazine, are placed. Most of these letters were intended for the editor of my articles, Dr. Conan Doyle, whose reinterpretations of my prose have led many to believe that both Holmes and myself are little more than imaginary characters. Some, however, sought out Holmes' assistance in the same manner as those letters directly addressed to our Baker Street apartment.

I do wish that Doyle had taken greater care in preserving these correspondences, but the gentleman was not as meticulous in his record keeping as I, and suffered from periods of neglect where he felt his writing career had been hampered by our agreement. A great many of Doyle's references have been lost or mislaid. In my own view, our adventures are responsible for his good fortunes, finding readers in many lands who might otherwise have had no interest in his historical and medical stories. While I am grateful to Doyle for proofing and editing of my articles, very often the published version would elicit criticism from their subject, who would often tut and shake his head whenever he failed to get my name wrong, or when the times and places described within of a story were woefully misrepresented. Eventually, in response to comments made during the time that Holmes was presumed dead, my companion chose to read these tales no more, dismissing them as a distraction, and as a gross distortion whose only purpose was to promote his consulting services to those with insufficient wit to solve problems for themselves.

Most of these letters came from the counties beyond London, or from countries like Poland, India and America, where the exploits of Sherlock Holmes have been

particularly popular. In most cases the distance involved and the delay in receiving this letters rendered them little more than useless, for any help we could have provided would arrive too late to be of practical value. In most cases letters deemed of any import would be immediately forwarded to Baker Street and a few cases did result, such as the affair of the devil's jawbone and the mystery of the man trapped in amber, but these were few and far between.

Many of these letters, however, have little to do with Holmes' cases, nor with the science of deduction. They are of a more personal nature. Scattered among the attempts to procure a signature and the requests for either Holmes' or, on one occasion my own hand, in marriage, I have found a large number of letters asking for more information about our backgrounds. Holmes' family history and upbringing are of particular interest, as are questions about the nature of my war wound and the legitimacy of my many marriages (it seems that many readers of Doyle's misinterpretations have deduced that I have had no fewer wives than King Henry VIII, a fact which both flatters and dismays). While I shall not approach these matters as a biographer would, relating intimate details and intruding upon those matters deemed too personal or sensitive to recount, I shall endeavour to provide an overview of my life and times with Sherlock Holmes, taking the opportunity to answer many of the questions posed by readers of the Strand.

On the nature of my relationship with Sherlock Holmes, it has been suggested that we had met prior to taking up lodgings together at 221B Baker Street. I can assure you, gentle reader, that this is not the case. Our first meeting followed quite quickly after my discharge from the Army where I served as an assistant surgeon for a period of some twenty months. I provided medical aid to British and Indian Troops during the Second Afghan War, where I was eventually assigned as Surgeon-Lieutenant to the Berkshires. I sustained my injuries aboard the relief aerostat Keane during the Battle of Maiwand in the year 1880. Downed by enemy rockets, the Keane crashed in mountains over the Panjshir Valley, and as senior surviving officer it took me some days to lead the survivors back to Kabul. These injuries were not extensive—some shrapnel was embedded along the left-hand side of my body, which also suffered minor burns—but they did leave me prone to the enteric fever that nearly killed me and succeeded in ending my army career. It was only the administration of a local cure—powdered cannabis leaves, mixed with sugar and fried in ghee with black pepper and poppy seeds—that rendered me well enough to be shipped home to recuperate. It was also, I am sure, the reason why my memories of the return home bear little relation to reality. It was an experience I would not care to repeat.

Sherlock Holmes had, by this time, already been in London lodgings for around five years, having left University early. Prior to that he had lived in Surrey until the death of his father, a retired army Captain, had chosen to settle upon retiring from service with the East India Company. He had spent a year experimenting with the art of deduction before he was invited to share rooms in Montague Street with a fellow called Ormond Sacker.

There is little I can recount of this period, for Holmes barely spoke of it. What fragments I have uncovered suggest that he was had fallen out with his eldest brother, Sherrinford, who ran the family's estates in Yorkshire, quite close to the town of Wetherby, and that his other brother was the only relative with whom he retained any contact.

Like his family, Holmes says little about his time with Sacker, and even less about the nature of their friendship, for I assume that they were friends. This came to an end more than a year before Holmes and I were introduced. What transpired between them, and what happened to Sacker if, indeed, he still lives, I have not been able to determine. What I do know is that Sacker had studied at the same University as Holmes, where they had first met. His ancestors had emigrated to

America in the wake of the highland clearances, and he was the of his family first to return to British shores where he became an engineer.

My friend's given name is Sherlock. It is not a made-up name or a pseudonym, and it is definitely not Robert, as one correspondent suggested. Similarly, my own given name is John, although my close friends and family call me James, which is a scotch tradition and nothing more sinister. Other details about my private life shall remain private, although I shall confirm, for the benefit of those who wish to know, that I was a bachelor when Holmes and I met. There was no Mrs Watson to greet me upon my return from the war, although I had previously been engaged to be married on two occasions and had a brief marriage, followed by annulment, prior to meeting with Miss Mary Morstan. I have been involved in two medical practices, a civil practice briefly shared with Dr Stamford in Farringdon, and my current practice, situated in Paddington.

Concerning our Baker Street apartment, Mrs Hudson is the landlady, not the housekeeper, and has a greater financial acumen than I. Fortunately for Holmes and I, her primary income has been her widow's fund, and her late husband's lease on 221B is held with the Peabody Estate of Marylebone. She lives for the most part on the ground floor of

the premises, and has had a number of other boarders in the second floor apartment that sits directly above our rooms. When her husband died, she chose to dismiss the household staff and take on many tasks herself, although the service she provides to Holmes and myself is out of choice and not duty.

As our case-load and popularity increased, the number of visitors to Baker Street made it necessary for Holmes to procure additional service, in the form of our loyal page boy. It was in the Christmas of 1886 that Holmes and the Irregulars rescued Billy and placed him into Mrs Hudson's care, and he has been an able and invaluable assistant ever since. His principal duty is to man the back door and to carry news to and from Holmes' many contacts as fast as his Bolton electric bicycle will carry him.

Outside of Baker Street, Holmes and I lead different lives, and it is rare for us to attend any kind of social occasion together unless it involves a case. While I earn a meagre sum as a medical practitioner from my consulting rooms in Kensington, what Holmes gets up to is much less predictable. His preference will always be for research based upon action and observation, either on the streets of London or locked away in whatever unused room is currently available. There are times when Mrs Hudson has indulged his use of the basement, the kitchen, the pantry and, when

vacant, the apartment upstairs. His current experiment involves a study of the various oils used to lubricate mechanical parts. He believes that just as the mud on boots can be used to determine where and when somebody has been walking, so too can traces of oil and grease be used to identify the make, model and purpose of the machine it comes from. While I expect a monograph to be announced shortly, I suspect he plans to use the information to demonstrate a level of expertise that will divert the attentions of the increasingly high number of engineers in the city from his poor practical knowledge of the profession.

Where in London Holmes may go will be entirely dependent upon his current obsession. At the time of writing his current idée fixe involves timing the transport routes and testing the connections across the city. All the changes of the last decade—the tar-grouted macadam thoroughfares, the pneumatic underground, the steam ferries, the electric carriages and the newly permitted aerostat moorings—have revolutionised the speed with which one can traverse and leave the city. Holmes believes it to be vital that, at least once per month, he revisits the copious notebooks into which he meticulously records the details of his journeys. On other occasions he may simply be found reviewing newspapers at the British Library, studying exhibitions at the British Museum, collecting book orders from Barnes of Melcombe Street or securing entry into private or forbidden collections such as that held at the Library of St. John the Beheaded in Holborn.

Of Holmes' other obsessions I suppose I should also pass comment. One such passion is music, and in particular the violin and the aether-violin, which has opened his eyes to the world of invention. Sherlock is an accomplished player, but the strings of his old violin did not produce the most enchanting sound. For many years he had refused to clutter his mind with science and technology, both of which he deemed as unnecessary in the art of detection. Then, during an evening concert in 1875 he saw the great virtuoso, Pablo de Sarasate, perform on the very first aether-violin. This had been specially constructed for him by the company of Siemens & Bain, and the sound so captivated Holmes that he immediately spent funds that had been set aside to pay for his final year at University to purchase the second.

Holmes has, over the years, acquired enough knowledge of the aether-violin that he has adapted is original to produce a greater range of haunting sounds which have, when played through an open window by the insomniac detective at three in the morning, made many a drunk teetotal. It was not until this year, and a chance encounter with a Stradivarius in a Jewish brokers' shop on the Tottenham Court Road, that

Holmes rekindled his love for the original instrument.

His other passion, thankfully set aside when he has a full case-load, is that of self-treating the bleaker moods that he dismisses as boredom and a lack of excitement.

My views are perhaps uncommon, and have drawn comment from the Strand's readers who suggest that my occasional references to my friend's use of stimulants seems overly critical, and that my opinions are often at odds with those of other general practitioners. I have been a follower Dr. Thomas Allinson's hygienic theory of medicine ever since he set up practice in Marylebone, and I have come to share many of his views regarding the dangers of excess and the frequent use of toxic drugs. My own experience of cannabis and opium have certainly influenced my belief in prescribing lower doses than many of my peers.

The approach taken by Sherlock Holmes reminds me of a medical school practice known as auto-experimentation, wherein a number of my fellow students took a variety of tinctures to observe their effects first-hand. I am certain that Holmes similarly dabbled with a number of stimulants before settling upon his preferred combination of coffee and cocaine-salts.

With regard to his consumption of coffee, Holmes' preference is for a strong Arab mixture that equates to some four grams of ground coffee

per cup, but which he brews by the potful. I assume that he acquired this habit from many late nights spent investigating the gambling dens and fencing operations that hide behind the respectable façade of the London coffee house. I, on the other hand, prefer a measure of whisky and soda.

Of Holmes' cocaine-salt dependence I have at least exerted some influence, and his preference is for the injection of a seven per-cent mixture pre-prepared by William Gulliver and Son of Lower Belgrave Street, although when in the countryside he will sometimes choose to smoke a brand of cannabis indica cigarette prepared by Gremault, of Paris. At home he prefers a pipe filled with his favourite black shag tobacco, while my own preferred cigarettes are Tiedemann's bird's eyes.

Which brings me, dear reader, to a final word concerning the life and times of a consulting detective. The majority of our excursions are within a short distance from the heart of London, and it takes a truly exceptional case, or one whose fees are paid well in advance, to draw us into the countryside or beyond. Our overseas investigations are usually at the invitation of the state or, at the very least, of the local authorities. There will always be exceptions, such as our recent voyage to the lunar colonies, but the time and distance involved will always need to be taken into account, as does the political climate of the country. Russia, for example, has tended to discourage the possibility of a visit by Holmes and myself, despite the popularity of my stories in that country.

JOHN H. WATSON M.D., 1889
Baker Street, London

THE INTERCEPTED LETTER
by Adem Rolfe

After all the excerpts, we present here the only complete story of this volume. Inspired, perhaps, by Poe's Purloined Letter, it jumps forward to a time when Holmes is absent from Baker Street, when Watson is forced to go it all alone:

"Nothing is more hateful to wisdom than excessive cleverness"
– Petrarch

It was upon the anniversary of the Reichenbach incident that I received a most unusual invitation to dine at the Diogenes Club with Mycroft Holmes. We had barely communicated since, save at a small private service where I saw, for the first time, the sense of brotherly responsibility that the elder Holmes must have felt about his brothers' demise. We did not—could not—discuss the events that had occurred there, and yet our shared loss now drew us together in the perfect silence that the club required of its members. Neither one of us acknowledged the presence of the other as, with our ruminations ended, the portly bureaucrat dabbed at his great chin with a serviette, and rose to lead me into the Strangers Room, where we might, finally, acknowledge each other.

"You must forgive me, Doctor Watson," said Mycroft, breaking his silence as he settled into the great leather chair reserved for his exclusive use, "for asking you to indulge me as you have. There are few men who knew my brother Sherlock as you and I, and only one other who shares the secret I am about to divulge."

While the precise the nature of his position was unspoken, it had become clear to me over the years that Mycroft Holmes served the interests of the British Government in all matters, and that this duty had brought the brothers into direct conflict on more than one occasion. One such conflict had ended at Reichenbach, and the heavy burden that now lay upon Mycroft's shoulders was, perhaps, to be shared. Reaching into the pocket of a large tweed jacket, his thick fingers closed around a worn letter which he laid upon the coffee table before me. It bore my name and the Baker Street address that Holmes and I had shared, on and off, for ten years.

"This was intercepted shortly after you moved into rooms with my brother. It was accompanied by a thick file which remains in my possession."

"Intercepted?" I paused for a moment. That Mycroft acted as Her

Majesty's cabinet noir I had known for some years, but that I might have been deemed important or dangerous enough to steal my post was quite a shock. "Isn't tampering with the post a crime under British Law?"

"When it isn't a matter of state security. This document was withheld in a vain attempt to protect my brother from the desperate chain of events that eventually followed—"

"May I see?" I said, picking up the letter. It was postmarked April, 1884, and appeared to be unopened.

"It is standard for such letters to be discretely opened and resealed before being returned to the mail. In this case it was deemed too sensitive to be returned to you. Until now."

"And the file that accompanied it?"

"That will always be too sensitive to share. This letter at least, while allegations are made, makes no incrimination."

Peeling open the lip of the envelope, I drew a slim sheet of paper from within.

"Ormond Sacker?" I said, noting the signature at the foot of the letter. I had recalled the name, in passing, as that of the fellow with whom Holmes lodged for a time before we met.

"Perhaps the only other man who knew Holmes as well as you or I. They were at college together, briefly, and later shared rooms in Montague Street."

"They were close?"

"Not exactly. The letter will explain all. If you will excuse me?"

Then, as silently as we had entered, Mycroft rose from his chair, and left the room. I hadn't even had time to sit down, and so I settled into the chair and began to read:

"My Dearest Doctor Watson, — I regret that our paths have not crossed, although without the circumstances of my disappearance your current circumstances may be very different.

My name is Ormond Sacker. It's unusual, I know, but that is what you get for being half-Scottish and half-American. Even worse when you've gone to ground for a few years and your name is so rare that rumours of your demise have become facts. Of course, if you are in possession of this letter that demise will have come to pass.

There will be an obituary. Not a long one, but something slipped into the Times by a grieving friend who will feel it is the least that he can do.

I use the terms grieving and friend somewhat loosely, because I doubt the man in question is capable of grief, and for all the time we spent together his idea of friendship was indoor marksmanship and refusing to share his tobacco. His name, by the way, is just as outlandish as mine.

Sherlock Holmes.

Brilliant mind, but cold as a fish most of the time, and as analytical as an electrical abacus. I hope that I might take some of the credit for the latter, just as he should take credit for some of my own quirks. I'd love to know how he feels about his fame,

particularly because they never seem to know whether to report on him in the society columns or on the news pages. Of course, he loathes society, and he shuns the news, even though most of the main stories have his footprints all over them, and no doubt he still loathes Scotland Yard taking all the credit for each crime that he solves.

But enough about Holmes, with whom you are as familiar as I. Let me tell you something of myself. This is my account, so it is only right that I focus on my own life; and upon its end.

I didn't know my father for most of my life. He met my mother when she was on tour. Myra Sacker (She was born Mairead, but that was too much of a mouthful for the stage) was an actress, or a dancer, depending upon whom you ask. He was passing through and, well, they got pretty well acquainted in a very short space of time. She was a showgirl, and barely a woman, so there was no way he could have kept in touch. She went on to do a lot of burlesque at Wood's Museum and Metropolitan Theatre in New York. I was twelve when she finally started answering questions about my father. Until then I had thought him to be the man I was named for, an Irishman called Ormond Brannigan, who had been with my mother for more than three years. Eventually though, during the fall season of '66, she wrote to him. It was not until two years later that he turned up to meet with me, and we were lucky not to have moved on. When he did arrive, he was keen to get me away from the show-life and into a proper school.

It turns out he was moneyed, and in a town like New York money buys more influence than righteousness. Before I knew what had happened I was being packed onto a steamer bound for Liverpool. Separated from my mother, I spent the next few years getting an education at the Edinburgh Academy and hating every minute of it. I missed her terribly, and was allowed to write, but the austerity of my father meant that no love was lost between us.

Upon leaving the Academy I faced two choices: medicine or engineering. For an educated scotchman these seemed to be the only choices, and my father was not just paying for my education, but also determining it. Medicine would have provided little opportunity for travel, and in my correspondence with mother I was keen to be reunited just as soon as I would be able. I therefore focused my talents upon engineering, and was able to secure a position within an English university.

Cambridge was very different from Inverleith, but the climate suited me and the work came easily. I studied hard and played hard, and it was here I first became acquainted with Holmes. For the whole of his first year he went unnoticed, as if he had blended in amongst us so well that he was simply invisible. For my part this changed when we both ended up joining three of the same sports clubs: boxing, chess and fencing. We were evenly matched, except at chess, where I found him easy to frustrate. Needless to say that we stayed in touch when we left University, and I invited him to share rooms with me in Montague Street. He was, I confess, my second choice, and it was based not upon the things we had in common, but entirely upon our mutual habit of staying silent and focused on our work for hours at a time.

For four years we shared those rooms, and as our separate interests would often overlap, so too did our mutual interest in problem solving. I'm not sure I can say with certainty which of us secured our first investigation, but the difference in our methods often brought us to a point of mutual agreement, which made our successes certain and our reputations solid. Of course ego, or vanity, led to several rather volatile clashes between us, but never at the expense of the case.

Living, as I now do, in the shadow of Sherlock Holmes' reputation, it is with some amusement that I recall the circumstances of our parting.

The year was 1880, and after some notable successes that included the shooting of Spring-heeled Jack, we came upon a case that divided us so completely that our paths would never cross again beyond its conclusion.

Perhaps I should begin by outlining my method. You will know that Holmes is very much the savant, relying upon his well rehearsed skills to observe and then, through a process of elimination, to deduce. In many cases he merely states the obvious, but his true skill lies in his ability to connect the obvious to the obscure. All actions have consequences, and our friend relies upon observing as many as possible and then using them like dots which, by joining them together, creates an image in his mind.

Where Sherlock is deductive, it is my preference is to be inductive. As an engineer I am in awe of the power of numbers, and of the way that statistics can be used to navigate the most probable chain of events given a particular scenario.

Take the humble bee, or the ant. Do we attribute them with the spirit of free will to explain how they might mark territories, build homes or gather nectar? We do not; nor do I attribute the human species with the conscious manipulation of its history to create the society in which we exist. The actions of the multitude, applied to the fulfilment of their instinctive needs, overcome obstacles which cannot be achieved by the individual. What separates men from these creatures is the power of the individual mind to conceive solutions that multiply the collective actions of the many. Just as a cannon gives a practised artilleryman power over a hundred spear-wielding natives, so too can one engineer's blueprint, applied by a thousand practised workers, make bridges and ships and rockets that overcome even the most resistant obstacles.

While neither method is perfect, Holmes and I often disagreed over which, ultimately, was the most effective. We chose to apply the argument to a social conundrum. Our penultimate case, the lifting of the killer fog, had led us to investigate the sulphurous yellow smog that enveloped London for just a few days, but whose claim on human life seemed immeasurable. There are estimates that between two and twelve thousand died of respiratory complications during the month that followed. You would have been overseas at the time, but the smog crippled traffic across the city. It hung so low upon the ground, and was so heavily laced with flakes of coal that masks were needed to navigate the streets. Holmes retreated to the laboratory with samples of the poisonous soup, while I began the process of triangulation and elimination based on a combination of meteorological records and trends in the import and export of coal into the city. We arrived at the same conclusion but from two very different directions, and our evidence was used to pave the way for clean air legislation and the wholesale adoption of incandescent lighting as an alternative to coal gas.

Where we differed was in our ultimate conclusion. While Holmes attributed the event, like the Great Stink of London years before, to a combination of political ignorance, industrial negligence and corporate greed, I voiced suspicions that these and a number of other, less prominent events, might represent a manipulation of circumstance on a monumental scale. The speed with which these so-called catastrophes were dealt with, and the emergence of great engineering projects on a size and scale never before considered, had led me to suggest the involvement of a directing mind. While Sherlock dismissed my theory, I rigorously pursued it, and my dedication took up so much time that I could no longer assist him with the more mundane cases that filled his days.

I was, I confess, completely obsessed with the theory which, instead of investigating directly, I determined to solve through statistical analyses. I compared the growth rates of companies that invested in new technologies, I cross-referenced board memberships and political affiliations, and I catalogued many seemingly unconnected industrial incidents whose outcomes were to stimulate the rise and wealth of British Industry. Somewhere I knew, at the centre of this great web of adversity and accumulation, sat a captain of industry whose influence might very well exceed that of even Gladstone and Disraeli at their peak.

There were harsh words on several occasions, and we parted company shortly after. Holmes vacated my Montague Street rooms to pursue his obsessions without the distractions of my own, and chanced upon Baker Street and an affiliation with your good self. I see from your accounts that his disposition is little changed, but that his attitude towards his fellow men has mellowed in your company.

With all of this in mind, I can perhaps unburden myself of the gravest concerns. Shortly after we went our separate ways, I moved to Birmingham, *where an engineering contract occupied my days, while my continuing investigations occupied the remainder of my waking hours. After four years I finally have a name for the man whose invisible touch steers us towards a future that I struggle to imagine. A future in which wars are conducted with weapons so powerful and so destructive that millions could die in the blink of an eye, where business aggressively leads and governments meekly follow, and where personal greed will replace the social conscience of the British Empire.*

Just having that name makes me a target, and knowing that I have his name will make him vengeful. Whether I am dead or disappeared this night, I must pass on the secret that I hold, and with it the record from which I drew my inescapable conclusions. Accompanying this letter is a file which I invite Sherlock to peruse at his leisure. To him I say this apply your own methods; within the file is a sealed note for your eyes only. It contains the name, but for the sake of our wager, I'll ask you not to open it until your own conclusions have been drawn.

Yours truly,
Ormond Sacker."

I sat, my jaw open, digesting the implications of the letter. In the early years Holmes was coy about his suspicions, and both I, and his brother, had dismissed these allegations as evidence of obsessive behaviour, or over-thinking. Only when the evidence stared us in the face did we at last believe Holmes' often fantastic hypotheses; and in all that time, Mycroft had known. He had done his duty—to steer his brother well away from his suspicions, and to keep any evidence that might confirm them at arm's length. He had, on more than one occasion, involved me in dissuading my friend from such fanciful thoughts; made me complicit in those matters which led to—

I screwed up the letter. I had a mind to throw it, in disgust, into the burning embers of the great open fireplace that graced the Strangers' Room. Instead I paused, plunging it deep into my pockets before rising and, in the Diogenes tradition, leaving without the utterance of a single word. Not, at least, until I reached the street.

"Moriarty!" I bellowed, unleashing my fury into the crisp night air.

WHAT IS STEAMPUNK ANYWAY?
by Adrian Middleton

It is entirely possible that, as a fan of Sherlock Holmes, this will be the reader's first brush with the steampunk genre. It is also entirely possible that the reader may have had a brief flirtation with early steampunk, and may be dipping his toes into modern steampunk for the first time. If so, it begs the question, what is steampunk?

Genre mutates; and the steampunk of the twenty-first century isn't what it was in the twentieth. It started out as a literary affectation, not even a sub-genre, and the name kind of stuck. With no real literary movement driving it, steampunk migrated into modern subculture, and became a something of a fashion statement for the well-to-do goth about town. That too changed, as even the non-goths and the not-so-well-to-do now find it an affordable fashion, and the steampunk movement has at last become a revolution, returning to its literary roots because, let's face it, the pen is a more enduring method of expression than corsets and goggles..

In literary terms, modern steampunk should perhaps be renamed 'steampulp', focusing as it does on tales of adventure and romance. Nothing wrong with adventure and romance, but there seems to be a dividing line between this and the desire by many to see a more socially conscious foray into the realms of Imperialist/Victorian social and cultural history. There may be room for both, but in the hard-nosed literary marketplace the lack of distinction between the two can rankle.

The original Steampunk stories were pure fantasy with a touch of laudanum-laced pseudo-historical licence. To be fair, the idea of punk as a reaction against the establishment wasn't particularly visible within those early stories, which were simply imitating the earlier Victorian fantasies of Burroughs, Haggard, Kipling, Verne, Wells et al. in what Locus Magazine originally referred to as the 'gonzo-historical' novel.

The 'founding four' steampunk novels were Tim Powers' *The Anubis Gates* (a time travel fantasy novel set in both the modern day and in an early 19th century where followers of the Egyptian gods are secretly at war with the British Empire), James P. Blaylock's *The Digging Leviathan* (Often discounted as a steampunk novel in favour of its successor, *Homunculus*, possibly because it was set in 1964. This was a comic science fiction adventure inspired in part by the works of Edgar Rice Burroughs while *Homunculus*, by contrast, was the first book to throw Victorian spaceships and the undead into the mix), K W Jeter's *Morlock Night* (a sequel, of sorts, to H G Wells' *The Time Machine*, this was the first of the so-called Powers/Jeter/Blaylock triumvirate novels. This and its successor, *Infernal Devices*, set the tone for most future steampunk tales), and the latecomer to the genre, William Gibson and Bruce Sterling's *The Difference Engine* (this book is often a honourable addition to the cornerstone books of the genre, probably because Gibson and Sterling were the founding fathers of Cyberpunk).

Of the original steampunks, Blaylock to the surreal and alternate world approach while Powers, using secret history, drew most on outsider culture, basing may of his Victorian underworld characters on Henry Mayhew's *London Labour and the London Poor*. In contrast, Gibson and Sterling introduced an alternate Victorian history theme, as sort of 'what if?' approach with its consequences rooted in post-modern hindsight.

Having been at the forefront of the earlier cyberpunk movement, it makes sense that it was Jeter who coined the term 'steampunk', although in doing so there is no real exploration of punk as a theme within the books themselves. Jeter's approach was to introduce themes now beloved of many modern urban fantasies. *Infernal Devices*, for example, played out the first clockwork automaton-as-antagonist storyline used in many later steampunk tales, and indeed it was whilst promoting this novel that the term came into being.

None of these genre classics fully explored the anti-establishment viewpoint, and their heroes were largely drawn from the scientist-outsider mould that became the standard for later stories. While the latter occasionally touch upon the anti-establishment viewpoint, they don't change the fact that most steampunk stories continue to revisit the 'scientific romance with hindsight' theme, or else offer glimpses of alternate histories inspired by historical possibilities.

If you were to compare the style and tone of these books to a pre-steampunk novel that defined itself as a 'scientific romance', such as Christopher Priest's *The Space Machine*, you would be hard-pressed to find much difference between them. Similarly, the first non-literary incursions into steampunk-before-it-was-in-vogue support this approach. Frank Chadwick's Space 1889 role-playing game caught the spirit of modern steampunk through the expansion of the British Empire and the lead up to a Worlds-war through adventures and conflicts between liftwood ships that traversed the aether between Earth, Venus and Mars. In computer games of the time similar adventures were being spun off by Lord British of Ultima fame, with his classic Martian Dreams. This concept of 'scientific romance' hardly evokes a punk edge, although the naïveté of the "Imperialist civilizers of lesser nations" must surely, in cotemporary fiction, reflect more upon the imposition of moral values than the Victorians themselves might ever have done. The heroes of scientific romance or Victorian fantasy are now, as they were at the time they were originally conceived in, firmly rooted within the Imperial middle or upper classes. It is still rare to see the working classes or the poor cast in any significant role, with the possible exception of the child urchin. But even when these appear, they are—like Oliver Twist—either the children of the fallen gentry or else—like Pip Pirrip in Great Expectations—they become the inheritors of some great fortune.

Alternate histories, by contrast, clearly should, and do, explore the consequences of the societal models they present, but that's more about the author than it is about the genre. Often they are merely vehicles for a new and fantastical world that couldn't possibly exist today, and the unique features of that world may be of more interest than how the little people are affected by it. Whatever steampunk now is or will become, the fact remains that it is driven by two things: who the publishers think are their target audience, and which

genres they want to fit their books into. The harsh reality is that most steampunk is not seen as particularly sabulous, but is treated more like light entertainment. This means that many uncomfortable historical truths will be glossed over in favour of the adventure.

Compare Verne with Dickens. The former is offering up pure escapism while the latter is consciously offering up a social commentary.

Compare Wells with Haggard or Kipling. The former considers the often negative consequences of scientific discovery, while the latter tell jolly good yarns that occasionally read as politically incorrect because time for the reader has moved on.

It is ultimately for the author, and not the tropes of a genre, to decide if they should offer up a gritty, historically accurate anti-Imperialist viewpoint or to simply emulate the language and ignorance of the Victorian Age. Social commentary with hindsight is perhaps the biggest 'new' perspective that can be brought to these stories. Dickens was, after all, a Victorian man, and as such even his social commentaries would have failed to accurately reflect women's suffrage and other experiences at the time. That doesn't mean it is seen as something that will sell a book to the modern audience. Right now that choice, for better or for worse, sits with the publisher. From a twenty-first century perspective, most mainstream steampunk is now provided through 'young adult' fiction. Bearing in mind that these books are being read by fifteen to twenty five year olds, there should be plenty of scope for a realistic, almost educational view of the Victorian age. It is up to those authors to decide if they wish to take such a risk.

Just so you that know, the steampunk adventures of Sherlock Holmes recounted here are set in a parallel world whose history has been subtly changed by the influence of Holmes' arch-nemesis, Professor James Moriarty. These stories are, primarily, told through the unabridged notes of Doctor Watson, and while the stories are often the same, we hope that they will delve deeper into the underbelly of the British Empire to paint a much more vivid and balanced picture than publishers of the nineteenth century would ever have allowed.

(This article originally appeared in a different form in #6 of the fanzine Andromeda's Offspring in February 2013)

STEAMPUNKING SHERLOCK
An Interview with the Authors

When we announced that we would be giving Sherlock Holmes a complete steampunk make-over, we took the opportunity to pose a few questions to the series' editor, Adrian Middleton, and to four of the authors—David McIntee, Mike Chinn, Damon Cavalchini and Jonathan Green—whose mash-ups of the original Holmes novels will launch the Moriarty paradigm series in late 2013.

What will makes the series different from the traditional gaslit mysteries we've previously been used to?

David: The steampunk elements, the focus on adventure, and... you know, actually that's one that needs to be answered with an "it just is, trust us," because so much of the specifics would be spoilers... but, also, to be honest, the Holmes canon was always a prototype of that genre, not just an example of it—and it's still Holmes, it's about these characters and their skill-set, not about bobbies on the foggy beat as the gaslit mystery ended up becoming. So why should it be that?

Adrian: The Holmes stories themselves evolved from detective adventures to clever mysteries to pulpier action. However, as long as Holmes the detective remains the centre of attention, the world he is in will happily revolve around him.

We've all seen and heard about *Pride & Prejudice and Zombies.* Doesn't a mash-up novel, mixing original text with new material, not undermine the integrity of the original?

David: There's certainly a danger of that if it's done badly, but, if it's done well, it can bring a lot of new interest, both in terms of making it more accessible or interesting to an audience from a different culture (and our 21st century culture is very different than that of, say, Victorian London), and of bringing in new readers who might then seek out the original.

Adrian: I was appalled when I first encountered the mash-up concept, especially because the early examples were so badly done; but then I often found myself appalled by how many original Holmes stories stray from the facts laid down in the canon, and I realised no subject matter is better for reinterpretation than Sherlock Holmes—Stephen Moffatt, Mark Gatiss and Guy Ritchie have all realised this.

David: People and cultures have always reinterpreted prior tales like this—every time a Shakespeare

play or classic opera is re-set into a different era or country, that's a mash-up on some level. Sometimes, though, it's just fun, or—in this case, I think—it's a natural outgrowth of the popularity of two distinct elements, which sort of make you wonder what would happen if you mixed them into a cocktail. Maybe it's two similar elements, and maybe it's two opposites, but it's a natural thing to wonder how they'd mix.

It just has to be done very carefully.

Jonathan: It would be all too easy to re-write *The Hound of the Baskervilles*, throwing in a few steampunk clichés here and there. However, that would be totally disrespectful of Sir Arthur Conan Doyle's accomplishments— the equivalent of sticking a few gears on a pair of boots and branding them 'steampunk'.

Instead, I want to make sure that the steampunk aspect becomes intrinsic to the plot, and that will involve quite a bit of head-scratching, I'm sure.

How can a story involving pulp action and adventure within a steampunk setting still be Sherlock Holmes?

Damon: Haven't you seen *Sherlock Holmes in the 22nd Century*? Or *Sherlock Hound*? Or even the Guy Ritchie movies?

Mike: The framing story will still be pure Holmes—simply expanded a little to allow for the new steampunk sensibilities to be fitted in. [In my

case] I can't help feeling that Conan Doyle broke loose a little in the Vermissa Valley section of *Valley of Fear*, effectively slotting a Western into the middle of a detective story (it's well known he wanted to expand his literary horizons and escape the Holmes straitjacket); I'll be doing much the same. And secret societies have been the staple of pulp fiction for years: at the centre of the original novel is a very secret criminal society (based on real events).

Damon: Conan Doyle himself summed it perfectly in *the Sign of Four* when he had Holmes criticise Watson for attempting to tinge his accounts with romanticism. At their heart, the Holmes stories are adventures. I'm simply following in Watson's footsteps and working a love-story or an elopement (we all know about Watson and Mary) into the fifth proposition of Euclid.

In steampunking the canon, we're bringing the entire world of Sherlock Holmes into our universe, not picking up a character, dumping him in a strange land and calling him Sherlock Holmes. The Holmes, and the Watson of *Sign of V* are the Holmes and Watson of the canon. Holmes hasn't suddenly become a mad inventor or taken up aqua-aerobics.

Besides, plenty of other people have already placed him into many different times and settings. Even most of the Basil Rathbone movies moved him out of Victorian times. Yet there are those who claim Rathbone is embodiment of Holmes. If you get the character of Holmes right, he can exist anywhere.

How do you feel about working with an alternative universe, and in particular one created by Holmes' arch-nemesis, Professor Moriarty?

Adrian: It's not an original concept, but it is a popular one. I can think of at least two prior occasions where Moriarty turned out to the the time traveller from H G Wells, and if Moriarty really is the most brilliant of mathematicians, then it makes sense that he, and he alone, can see the probabilities and change them. His transformation of the world is technological after all, not biblical.

Damon: I love it. The special thing about this is that we are working in an expanded version of the canon. Not just the characters but Conan Doyle's stories. At its core, this is still *the Sign of Four* but in a bigger world, a world with layers upon layers. While these stories are all standalone, they connect with each other rewarding the person who reads all of them while still being great fun for the person who picks up a single book to sample.

As for Moriarty, he's the great shadow, the spider in his web. In these stories, we get to see the web. He has a purpose. A great and terrible purpose which will surprise and challenge people's expectations.

Besides who wouldn't want to share a world with people like Adrian, David, Mike and Jonathan? Some of the ideas being thrown around are breathtaking and can't wait to have an inside view as they teased together. And the next group of writers are already Toby-like chasing our scent.

A mash-up must be very different to writing a straight adventure or even a standard Holmes pastiche. What have the main challenges been?

Mike: One, resisting the temptation to fiddle with the canon material too much: putting in too much of my voice, as it were; two, getting a late 19th century sense of language and attitudes: Conan Doyle used a much wider vocabulary than we're used to; making my literary voice match his is fun (and rewarding: I get to employ words and meanings that would never pass in a story set in the 21st century).

Adrian: To better edit mash-ups, I've had to learn about the process from scratch, writing mash-ups of my own and learning the pitfalls before the authors do. That way I can at least assist them with some authority and experience. What I learned was that Doyle used ambiguous language all the time, and it can be tempting to tie up all the loose ends he left dangling. That might not leave much space for new storylines.

Another interesting challenge is the

ubiquity of airships in steampunk. Once they exist, earlier and more efficiently than in the real world, they take over. Every transport scene (Holmes loves his hansom cabs), every journey and every chase creates opportunities, and the writers will invariably take them.

Are you a fan of Holmes? Have you written for him before? How were you introduced?

Mike: This is the first time I've written Sherlock Holmes fiction of any kind—though I've often imagined taking a shot. I have the *Penguin Complete Sherlock Holmes* of course; and several anthologies of new Holmes fiction in a variety of genres and sub-genres (straightforward detective fiction, Holmes against the supernatural, or Lovecraft's Mythos creatures, etc.), so you could certainly say I was a fan.

David: Yeah, like, I suspect, most people my age I grew up on BBC2 always showing the Rathbone/Bruce series in the run-up to Christmas, and totally loved them—in fact I still do, I'll watch them whenever they turn up, usually on TCM these days.

Having been hooked by those, I went and read the original stories—must have been in my early teens, I guess—and then along came the Jeremy Brett series at about the same time, and that was fantastic too.

Mike: My first memory of the great detective was Douglas Wilmer playing him in black and white BBC adaptations (no idea how far back that was!); he was replaced by the great Peter Cushing—though I believe Nigel Stock played Watson in all of the episodes. And in the great debate I come down firmly on the side of Jeremy Brett. As a writer I try to imagine him speaking the dialogue in my head: if it sounds right, then I think I've just about nailed it.

Damon: Being the convict of the pack, I bring a criminal perspective that is extremely useful in writing Moriarty. Besides Sherlock Holmes often travelled aboard and he is as loved 'down under' as he is at home. Holmes' London has always been a fictional retreat for me. [In Australia] it is 38.3 degrees Celsius in mid-January. Which is slightly warmer than in the UK and not at all like Holmes' pea-souper cloaked London. Even now I regularly visit the world of Sherlock Holmes with Watson and Conan Doyle's occasionally sparse descriptions as my travel guide. The Holmes' stories were a universe away for the imagination of a young man and they remain a much loved pleasure for an older one. They were full excitement and mystery and some great writing I mean who else but Holmes could describe Inspector Jones as being as 'tenacious as a lobster' and still be taken completely seriously?

David: I have written Holmes and Watson before, actually—both in a still-to-be-finished radio play, and

they make anonymous large cameos in *Destination Zero*, a book I wrote in the Final Destination franchise.

Jonathan: It will be [my first Holmes story], strangely enough, although it won't be my last. When Abaddon Books were still accepting open pitches for Pax Britannia novels, somebody did pitch one that featured Sherlock Holmes. But, in the end, it wasn't to be.

Damon: I remember writing a very bad Sherlock Holmes pastiche to be performed by my English class when I was about 11 or 12. It was another of those stinking hot days and there were five of us who had to perform this 'mini-play'. Naturally I played Holmes and somehow avoided heatstroke in my makeshift deerstalker (I have no idea what my mum made the costume out of but I do remember it was slightly warm). This early work grew and eventually I created my own 'Holmes-like' character who has appeared in a couple of short stories.

You could say Sherlock (and Doctor Who) helped inspire to me write. Doctor Who made me love the broad brushstrokes of fiction and imagination while Sherlock Holmes taught the power of a fantastic short story. These weren't vignettes or standalone scenes. They were whole novels squeezed into a few pages. And, on a personal level, [Holmes] is the reason I wanted to learn the violin at school. Okay, it became a viola when my teacher realised I

could read the alto clef but the reason for me picking it up was the same.

Adrian, how important is world-building to these stories?

Adrian: Vital. A shared world starts and finishes with the bible, which is just a collection of vague ideas. We bounce these around, throw in some more facts and ideas, throw in some research and... it just grows. The authors have literally shaped the world in which these stories are set, encouraging each other to flesh out popular ideas, and reining each other in when something threatens to disrupt things. I can guarantee that the steampunk world we have created will be more than complementary to Doyle's London.

David, will Study be the same detective story, or will there be a new mystery for Holmes and Watson to solve?

David: The original story will still be there in it, but there'll be more to it—imagine it as the unedited version, before Watson cut it down for publication in the Strand. So... both. The same and new!

Mike, how he you be able to transplant Holmes from the the foggy streets of London to a steampunk colony on the far side of the moon?

Mike: In the original *Valley of Fear*,

the novel was split in two sections: the first dealing with a murder at Birlstone Manor and narrated by Watson in classic style; the second some two decades earlier in a mining community in the USA. It doesn't take much of a leap to transplant a bunch of frontier miners onto an even further frontier: the Moon—a Moon claimed and colonised by the British Empire.

The fun comes in imagining how 19th century spacesuits would look, how a technology based around steam could function in a near-vacuum; indeed, knowing how low down on a list of priorities safety would be I think the burgeoning colony would be populated with outlandish (and dodgy) machinery which would most likely never be operated on Earth.

I also asked myself what an American—and a member of a US police organisation at that—is doing in a British-owned colony and satellite. The answer to that pretty much gave me the angle for the re-imagined novel.

Jonathan, Hound was the most gothic of the Holmes adventures, and the story keeps you wondering if the resolution is supernatural or grounded in reality. Will you be doing the same?

Jonathan: Absolutely! I believe that it's the supernatural aspect of the story (whether it really is supernatural or not) that makes Hound the most memorable of all the Sherlock Holmes

canon and the consulting detective's most well-known adventure. To remove that questionable paranormal element would be to lose a vital part of the story.

And how does helping to build a shared fictional universe compare to creating one of your own?

Jonathan: Both bring their own challenges. Everything that exists within the world of Pax Britannia is there because I put it there, or because I agreed to its inclusion. However, the down side of that is that it's a lot of hard work!

Working as part of a group, and making sure everyone's ideas and opinions are listened to and valued, involves another skill set altogether. But when a group of like-minded people get together and bounce ideas off one another, who knows where they might end up taking an idea?

This project is a perfect example. It's going to be a very exciting venture. As Holmes himself would say, the game is afoot!

Damon, the original Sign had four antagonists, after whom the story was named. Does the V signify a fifth?

Damon: Ah. This V. He's just this guy, you know. V is many things to many people. A name. A place. A number. A letter. A date. A man in a porcelain mask looking for a date on Guy Fawkes night. The one thing I can tell you is that it is not an alien lizard disguised as human while trying to take over the world (at least not in this draft).

Conan Doyle himself was ambiguous about how many people should be involved. *The Sign of Four* (or as it was originally published, *the Sign of the Four*) was at one point going to be the Sign of the Six, hinting at a bigger, untold story. Forget about the V, you have no idea how long I agonised over whether to keep the 'the' in the title. Eventually I left it out because it is more mysterious.

In the end, I guess you are going to have to wait and read the book to find out.

Creating a shared world for multiple authors is a daunting task, and you've already commissioned eight novels and a couple of short stories. Where do you see this going?

Adrian: I came into this with a fear of reading Sherlock Holmes steampunk where the character might be the same but the setting wasn't right for Holmes. By working with a team of writers whose stories overlap, they fill in most of the gaps themselves. If we're going to put all of this effort into creating a believable steampunk world, then we might as well get plenty of use out of it.

My main goal is to produce an entire series of steampunk mash-ups based on the original Holmes canon of 56 short stories and 4 novels. In between those stories there is scope for original fiction, and in the world that surrounds Holmes there are opportunities for the concept to grow beyond just Sherlock Holmes.

The canon will provide a framework for new stories to be introduced. In doing so it sets dates, resolves inconsistencies and fleshes out a whole new world history. We know Holmes is popular, and I have faith in the quality of the end result. I can therefore take the leap of faith that says I will be releasing an ongoing series of tête bêche books that contain one mash-up of an original Holmes story and an original steampunk pastiche. In addition we've looked at a couple of H G Wells stories, using them to add some context to the setting.

HOLMES AND MORIARTY
A Steampunk Perspective

Written by Adrian Middleton, Mike Chinn, Theresa Derwin, David and Lesley McIntee, the following essay was presented to the University of London's Sherlock Holmes: Past & Present conference, held at the Institute of English Studies, Senate House, London in June 2013. It outlines our observations as an independent publisher, and as writers, about the impact of post-modern literature and the contemporary steampunk genre has had on modern characterisations of Sherlock Holmes and Professor Moriarty, and on how we determined what approach we should take, both in re-imagining the character and in restoring the relevance of the original canon.

The Abstract

The emergence of post-modern literature and the contemporary steampunk genre since the early 1980s have significantly influenced modern characterisations of both Sherlock Holmes and his arch-nemesis, Professor James Moriarty. By divorcing these characters from their original context within a canon of detective stories, they have been reduced to useful ciphers adopted by film and television, and within both graphic fiction and literature. Sherlock Holmes is more recognisable, for example, by a deerstalker, a meerschaum pipe and a catchy misquote, than by the setting and the methods that originally made him famous. Similarly, Professor Moriarty has become little more a template for the stereotypical evil genius driven by an abstract desire to conquer the world.

Using experience we have gained through researching, developing and collaborating to create a steampunk re-imagining of the original Sherlock Holmes canon, and with reference to the original Sherlock Holmes canon and selected primary sources, we will argue that the transplantation of Holmes and Moriarty into different genres such as gothic romance, intertextual pastiche, steampunk parody and modern drama have significantly undermined the essence of the character, and that only by re-imagining the original novels and stories from a modern perspective can both character and canon be reconnected.

The Presentation

It is our assertion that post-modern literature has encouraged the elevation of the character of Sherlock Holmes over the original body of work presented by Doyle.

We further assert that the rise of the contemporary steampunk movement, and its associated literary genre, have widened the degree of dissociation between character and canon.

We would argue that the transplantation of Holmes and Moriarty into different genres such as gothic romance, intertextual pastiche, steampunk parody and modern drama have significantly undermined the essence of the character, and that only by re-imagining the original novels and stories from a modern perspective can both character and canon be reconnected.

By divorcing these characters from their original context within a canon of detective stories, they have been reduced to useful ciphers adopted by film and television, and within both graphic fiction and literature. Sherlock Holmes is more recognisable, for example, by a deerstalker, a meerschaum pipe and a catchy misquote, than by the setting and the methods that originally made him famous. Similarly, Professor Moriarty has become little more a template for the stereotypical evil genius driven by an abstract desire to conquer the world, defined only by being the intellectual and moral antithesis of a given heroic figure.

As Scott Brown of Wired Magazine argued in 2009, it was the Holmes canon that largely inspired the concept of fandom and fan-fiction, despite not being named as such (the counter-argument is that fan-fiction had, to some degree, started with The Odyssey, and later with American copies and sequels to H.G. Wells' *War Of The Worlds*). Emerging in response to Holmes's death in *The Final Problem*, the rise of the Holmes pastiche mirrored the wider growth of detective fiction, with many characters, such as Hornung's Raffles and Leblanc's Arsene Lupin, being inversions of Doyle's creation. In this period the hunger for Holmesian fiction was barely fed by 56 short stories and a handful of novels. Copycat detectives like Sexton Blake and Solar Pons soon emerged, and Holmesian societies like the Baker Street Irregulars fuelled the desire to capitalize upon the popularity of Holmes in new adventures.

Perhaps the earliest treatment of Holmes in a post-modern context lies in the works of John Kendrick Bangs. The concept of a fictional dead detective interacting with historically dead celebrities takes little more than the trope of Holmes, divorced both from Watson and Victorian London. Although written as satire, with the full approval of Doyle himself, Bangs' Associated Shades stories heavily influenced the works of Philip José Farmer, whose own post-modern literary conceit is the Wold Newton Universe, in which all larger-than life fictional characters can trace their origins, through evidence based on shared physical and mental characteristics of fictional characters, back to a historical meteorite crash in 1795. The conceit was an easy one to make, because most fictional characters are connected by authors' jokes or 'easter eggs' hidden within the original texts.

Theatre, film and television have similarly contributed towards the myth of both Holmes's character and also that of Moriarty. Here, when we refer to the myth of Holmes and Moriarty, we are talking basically about myth as a false, superficial image of Holmes which has been perpetuated through the years, and divorces him from canon. This is because there is definitely a mythological/archetypal background to Holmes's original character. We would argue that he fits right into that line of archetypal Magus/Scientist figures in 19th century literature, like Frankenstein, or Jules Verne's professors. Moriarty fits the bill for his alter ego. So divorcing them from canon has lost that background and made them into much more one-dimensional figures.

The trappings of William Gillette shaped perceptions of the Holmes character independently of the content of the novels and short stories, and over time other actors and productions have similarly built the myth. Holmes's drug dependency, for example, is considerably overinterpreted, reaching a zenith with tales such as Nicholas Meyer's *The Seven Per-cent Solution*, which

portray simple character traits as physical and psychological handicaps. Similarly, Holmes's ambivalence towards women, his portrayal as a possible Asperger's or epilepsy sufferer in BBC's Sherlock, and his portrayal as a heavily tattooed recovering addict in Showtime's *Elementary* have similarly distanced the character from the original stories. In Sherlock, the detective is presented with character flaws which are elevated to physical defects. Cumberbatch's Holmes is quick to assure us that, "I'm not a psychopath. I'm a high functioning sociopath—do your research!"

In the 2009 Sherlock Holmes film with Robert Downey Jr, the relationship between Holmes and Watson has become comedic and Holmes's addictions turn him into a full blown 'unhygienic' addict. This short excerpt of dialogue from the film, expounds upon this:

Sherlock Holmes: You've never complained about my methods before.
Dr. John Watson: I'm not complaining.
Sherlock Holmes: You're not? What do you call this?
Dr. John Watson: I never complain! How am I complaining? When do I ever complain about you practicing the violin at three in the morning, or your mess, your general lack of hygiene, or the fact that you steal my clothes?

Since the post-modern era emerged from the ashes of the Second World

War, the brief flirtation of Basil Rathbone's Holmes with Nazi saboteurs aside, the great detective became a historically-fixed character associated with Victorian London. This, in spite of the fact that his adventures often related to the wider world, educating Doyle's readership as to the workings of the East India Company, the activities of the Mormons and the Ku Klux Klan in America, and the existence of negrito tribes in Malaysia. This vivid portrayal of the wider world from the armchair of a Baker Street study itself influenced many preconceptions about the Victorian era, which has in some quarters become more synonymous with the world evoked by Doyle than by the historical period recorded in history books. It should perhaps also be noted that while Doyle was writing about what was, to him, contemporary, his stories actually continued to be written well in the 20th Century (Casebook being published between 1921-27).

An example of such misconceptions can be illustrated by the inclusion of an Andaman islander in *the Sign of Four*. Its brief description of a Malaysian negrito perhaps embedded the concept of the blowpipe-wielding pygmy beloved of boys own stories, and yet, far from being three-feet tall, the only Andaman islander measured at that time was five feet three inches tall. By contrast, Long Liz, the tallest of the acknowledged Jack the Ripper victims, and notable for being a tall woman, was exactly the same height.

It was not until the 1980s, however, that the nature of the game changed. Just as Doyle had influenced the post-modern concept of the Victorian era, so too had Wells and Verne. The introduction of Vernian and Wellsian elements into the cinema of the 1970s did not just give rise to the early Steampunk movement, but also changed the nature of Holmes's portrayal, both in the cinema and, later, in literature. The Loch Ness submarine from *The Private Life of Sherlock Holmes* was perhaps the start, while Spielberg and Chris Columbus's *Young Sherlock Holmes and the Pyramid of Fear* took the cinematic Holmes away from canon and into the realms of supernatural adventure and scientific romance.

The Holmes pastiche matured with its adoption by other genres like science fiction and horror. During the 1980s this bled into popular culture, with stories where Holmes travels through time, either by Wellsian methods or by cryogenesis. *Star Trek: The Next Generation* set a benchmark with the appearance of Data as Holmes and Moriarty as a hologram, in the episodes *Elementary, My Dear Data* and *Ship In A Bottle*. At this point the characters had achieved a life beyond both canon and genre, and the disassociation of Holmes was complete. Cross-genre fiction blossomed as a vehicle for Holmes and, perhaps even more, Moriarty. In stand-alone fiction by the likes of John Gardner and Kim Newman, Moriarty has stood on his own merits, and, reflecting the conceits of Bangs and Farmer, has appeared in Alan Moore's post-modern graphic novel *The League of Extraordinary Gentlemen*, and its subsequent film.

Enter steampunk.

Where Doyle and Verne and Wells influenced film and early steampunk literature, so too has the mutation of steampunk influenced interpretations of Holmes. To be honest, Steampunk literature never quite took off like its elder sibling Cyberpunk, and it was the emergence of the steampunk aesthetic, focused around fashion and social interaction, that the second wave of steampunk literature—which for the purpose of differentiation we will call steampulp—emerged.

Steampulp has been embraced by the publishing industry, the film industry, and the fashion industry; and now, having usurped the mantle of steampunk, it is being embraced by Sherlock Holmes. Indeed, by the time of the Guy Ritchie reinterpretation, which recycled and updated many fantastical plot elements from *The Assassination Bureau Ltd*, it was a specific phrase, uttered in any number of anecdotal discussions: "Sherlock Holmes is Steampunk."

Sherlock Holmes is no more steampunk than sticking goggles on a top hat or wearing a cog brooch. But, just as steampunk is a modern retrospective that reflects upon tales of scientific romance, so too has Sherlock Holmes become a modern retrospective, about the tropes associated with the character. The deerstalker, the inverness cape, and the meerschaum pipe on the one hand, and the Asperger's and the drug addiction on the other. Although new Holmes stories appeared up to 1927, August 2014 will mark the centenary of Holmes's last canonical adventure, *His Last Bow*.

When faced with a statement that "Holmes is Steampunk" over a pint in a pub, as is most often the case, how does one refute such a statement? The academic argument is straightforward.

First, define steampunk.

Steampunk is a sub-genre of science fiction that typically features steam-powered machinery, especially in a setting inspired by industrialized Western civilization during the 19th century. Therefore, steampunk works are often set in an alternative history of the 19th century's British Victorian era or American "Wild West", in a post-apocalyptic future during which steam power has regained mainstream use, or in a fantasy world that similarly employs steam power.

Then define Holmes (which could take all day given the variety of literary and media representations of the icon).

Then point to the difference.

Unfortunately, neither is so easy to pin down. Steampunk was a literary

conceit which is now an aesthetic movement that shares little more than a name with its precursor; and Holmes? Holmes, as we have established, is now an iconic figure that stands apart from the stories that introduced him.

As writers, we use an expression, "show, don't tell". This usually means don't simply state something as fact, use your fiction to illustrate it. Writing original steampunk with Holmes would not prove our point. The only way to see that Holmes is not steampunk, is to show people

what Holmes as steampunk would look like. We therefore set out to capture the essence of the Holmes canon, as opposed to the Holmes icon, and this led us to the modern concept of a mash-up.

By framing an original Holmes story in a steampunk world, we can retain the essence of the canon, and better still, we can tell people to read our books, then read the original stories, and they will know the difference between Sherlock Holmes and steampunk.

INVENTING MORIARTYTECH
Steampunk technology through a Holmesian lens

Half the fun of creating a steampunk world is making stuff up, and any contemporary story will be brimful of giant babbage engines, clockwork cars, steam-powered robots, electrical ray guns and, of course, airships. The strategic application of cogs and goggles, while more a fashion statement than a piece of sound technical advice, is often seen as the defining characteristic of a steampunk world.

When conceiving of a such a place, the first question to address is what kind of playground are we in? Is it a fantasy world with a steampunk aesthetic? Is it the real world with discrete new technology and inventions that only the lucky few are aware of? Is it a re-imagining of the real world, and if what period is it set in? The modern era with a retro-steampunk feel, or the original Victorian era but with an overtly steampunk vibe.

In the case of the Moriarty paradigm. We know two things:

- that the stories are set in the Victorian period when Sherlock Holmes was active;
- that it is an alternate world apparently 'created' by Professor Moriarty

But it is the adaptation of a common Sherlock Holmes axiom that provides our clearest steer in embracing the steampunk aesthetic: if you eliminate the impossible, whatever remains, however improbable, can be invented.

How and why this world was created will be explored through the books and short stories, but it makes sense that this isn't so much a Victorian era full of modern technology, but rather one in which that era's full potential might be achieved. Things that could have been around back in the late nineteenth century will be making appearances as the stories progress. It is the technology itself that will fuel historical change, and in the first instance any new technology emerges as a direct result of Moriarty applying his understanding of science and history to the world in which he finds himself.

We do know that time travel will be involved, so lets assume that everything that existed when Moriarty was active in the traditional Holmes universe might be available to him in this steampunk alternative some thirty years earlier. Let us also assume that his preferences are for introducing the technology needed to ensure the rapid progress of communications, construction, environmental technology, medical equipment, rocketry, transportation engineering and weaponry to further

his plans. On this basis we can imagine what sort of technology will appear and when.

Communications

Imagine the genius of Tesla and Marconi backed by the hindsight of Moriarty. The battle of the currents would end very differently, and the telephone of 1876 could be followed by the portable wireless teslaphone of 1882.

The roll-out of wireless power in the Victorian age would be transformative. Telegraphs would become electrographs (or, once branded, Teslagraphs), and the fax machine would emerge as the Teslavizor, and teletext-style newsfeeds could be created by Teslatype, with whole documents and still images being electrically transmitted through the wireless medium; the landscape might positively hum as directed electrostatic beams project their power up to passing airships.

Computers

As a mathematician, Moriarty would do more than just appreciate the difference engines of Charles Babbage; he would embrace them. Similarly, he could embrace Otlet's World Brain, a device (launched in 1898 by the Repertoire Bibliographique Universel) which converts information stored on index cards into electric signals. In a Tesla-powered world where such information could be wirelessly transmitted, an electric web of connected computers could emerge as a reality long before the birth of Tim Berners-Lee.

Construction

New materials would emerge quickly, and the spirit of a British Empire unchecked by the wars of the twentieth century would fuel growth before decent planning laws existed, and before the consequences of such fast-paced advances might be fully realised. Towers would be built taller, shafts deeper, and things cautiously approached in the twentieth century, like mining and quarrying, might spread unchecked to meet the demand of new housing, particularly as the rapid growth of industrial centres would encourage high levels of immigration as much as a century sooner than in the real world. The Midlands in particular might spread unchecked, scarring and swallowing up much of the countryside long before the road network collared and tamed it.

Imagine a landscape, already riddled with unsafe mining tunnels, where new mining methods similar to modern 'fracking' are introduced. The famous Aberfan disaster, where a coal-heap plunged down a Welsh hillside and buried a school playground, might pale into

insignificance when the first mining village collapses into a vast crater filled with chemically poisoned seawater pumped into the tunnels under high pressure.

Environmental Technology

Pollution would be a major issue. The Great Stink of 1856 and the Killer Smog of 1880 would be just two incidents out of many that might cripple London for weeks at a time and encourage campaigns for clean air and better sanitation. While it sounds grim, this rapid pace of change would almost be exclusive to the British Empire, with only America, Russia and Germany capable of catching up. So many dangers would raise the social consciousness, and while the political machine would struggle to catch up quite so easily as in the modern era, it would be much easier for Victorian philanthropists and entrepreneurs to take direct action, and product testing would be ignored as new solutions were manufactured in the hope of providing solutions.

What might emerge from such zeal? Selenium boilers, perhaps? Imagine vast solar panels fitted to high-flying aerostats or laid out across the deserts of British Egypt and East Africa to generate enough power to industrialize a continent. Or maybe siphonic nucleation, a rain-making process used to green the Sahara Desert. Imperial enthusiasm might see water siphoned from the Mediterranean and Red Seas high into the atmosphere where a sprinkler system creates heavy clouds over the desert.

Medical Technology

Medicine advanced quite rapidly during the nineteenth century, and there is little that might be subject to change other than the less moral exploitation of its developments.

In the wake of resurrectionists like Robert Knox, the science of transcendent anatomy might see the application of drugs and mechanical appliances to the enhancement of the human body. Imagine devoting science to keeping soldiers on the battlefield, or to building machines capable of thrusting men into increasingly hostile environments such as on top of mountains, deep beneath the sea, high up in the stratosphere and even on the moon. Science in service of the Empire.

Pneumatic chemistry, a specialist field of scientific research abandoned in the early nineteenth century, responsible for the discovery and creation of various gases, would be seen as the key to discovering and manufacturing the lighter than air compounds that would revolutionize the aerostat industry. Without its abandonment, the science of molecular biology would rise much sooner, and the horrors of chemical warfare might loom large in India, the Crimea and the Franco-Prussian War.

Transportation Engineering

You can't have a steampunk world without airships, and the biggest change in transport must surely be the emergence as the airship as the dominant feature of the landscape. The standard model to emerge is the aerostat—a (usually tethered) non-rigid or semi-rigid envelope filled with hot air or, in a fictional context, steam. Without too much innovation, early investment and adoption could transform the landscape, bringing air travel into direct competition with the slightly more mature railways and canals.

Politics would inevitably influence how aerostat transportation might work, and it is likely that insurers and transport magnates would influence the thinking of parliament, allowing only passenger vessels to fly untethered, while tethered cargo packets would need to ply their routes along the travel routes established by the canals and the railways. The railways would maintain their advantage of carrying heavy cargo, but the canals, freshly laid, would be under threat. Harsh lobbying would doubtless have made the towing of tethered aerostat trains, in which a string of tethered aerostats trail behind, an inevitability. For a licence fee of course...

The types of gas used would become variable, with some bold experiments with helium and ammonia, and the development of aerial impellers similar, perhaps, to jet engines, sucking air into the main structure and ejecting it at speed as a means of propelling the vehicles forward.

In a novel twist, air-mail might travel much more slowly than surface mail, especially during the early years.

And you can forget parachutes as they, like balloons, drop vertically, and this would leave little room for escape. The concept of the kite-shaped gliders or 'aerovanes' would make much more sense when fleeing or otherwise deploying from a damaged aerostat.

On the ground, hybrid trains using a combination of steam and electricity might quickly become commonplace, while pneumatic tunnelling could speed up the creation of London's underground and could also make the dream of a submarine tunnel beneath the English Channel a reality; but the real revolution would be on the streets.

The electric bicycle would easily become the most common and affordable mode of assisted transport in the Victorian era, particularly favoured by inner-city doctors, vets and postmen. Pavements would become cycleways while cobbled streets would change little until the rise of the MotoCar. Just because steam changes things doesn't mean that motorised carriages won't be

necessary. They get a whole decade-or-so of development benefit from everything else that's going on, so the steam-powered carriage, the gas-powered carriage, the electric carriage and the petrol engine would all end up competing and cross-fertilizing each other. Karl Benz would end up designing carriages for his previous employer, Mannheim, so the big car of 1888 (as driven by the King of Bohemia) would be The Mannheim-Benz. There would doubtless be lots of names for the different vehicles in a non-standardized environment (MotoCar, for example, is simply a contraction of the term 'motorized carriage' which excludes steam-powered cars as they use engines, not motors). One oddity would be that tyres come somewhat later to the party, so alternatives (and alternative names like treads, cushions or dampers) would be in use, while the grinding iron rims of these monstrosities would devastate the cobbled victorian roads and force the early use of macadam roads in major cities like London, Birmingham and Manchester.

Rocketry

The early emergence of rocket science, while uncertain, could well be a priority for Moriarty, the man who wrote Dynamics of an Asteroid and whose primary discipline is mathematics. Airships would make the evolution of the Hale rocket into deadlier ordnance a real possibility, and no steampunk world would be complete without making efforts to reach the moon.

Weaponry

This is the world of Sherlock Holmes, so one thing is certain. Long distance pneumatic projectile rifles like that used by Sebastian Moran would be in regular use, perhaps as the weapon of choice for snipers and assassins. Chemical weapons would be in danger of being deployed; and other, more science fictional weapons, from electrostatic beam emitters, hydraulic, magnetic and pneumatic cannons, and radium rays would all be just around the corner. In such a world, guns would be bigger, armour would be thicker, and explosives would be more devastating.

For all of these great inventions, there is one we know will appear: Moriarty's Time Machine. Bringing him from the familiar world of Sherlock Holmes (what we call the Holmes paradigm) into a past where his vast intellect and knowledge of the future will create a new history (the Moriarty paradigm) in ways the reader can yet imagine.

CONTRIBUTORS

DARREL BEVAN : Colourblind, Darrel is a portrait and figure illustrator who, due to colour blindness, specialises in graphite illustration—mainly on black and white images. When he isn't producing photorealistic pencil drawings, he teaches.

DAMON CAVALCHINI, based on our deductions, lives in Australia. He is right-handed, slightly overweight, works in an office and he likes to pretend he has more hair than he does. A lifelong fan of the canon, he grew up with Basil Rathbone before switching allegiance to Jeremy Brett. Although he does retain a fondness for Tom Baker's Hound. Sign of V is Damon's first published novel.

MIKE CHINN has been a Holmes fan since childhood and has written horror, fantasy and science fiction for years, publishing over forty short stories and edited two anthologies for The Alchemy Press; the same imprint published a pulp adventure collection. He has also scripted SF and fantasy comics for DC Thomson's late-lamented Starblazer digest and the Beano as well as two how-to books on writing for comics.

JONATHAN GREEN has more than forty books to his name, from Fighting Fantasy gamebooks to numerous Black Library and other books based on such diverse properties as Doctor Who, Star Wars and the Teenage Mutant Ninja Turtles. He is the creator and author of the Pax Britannia series for Abaddon Books, and still finds time to live in West London with his wife and their two children. To find out more about his current projects visit www.jonathangreenauthor.com.

DAVID McINTEE is a full-time writer with twelve Doctor Who novels, several other tie-in novels, original novels, media studies books, history and mythology books for Osprey, and a Star Trek novel to his name. He has written comics, and several radio plays, including a Sherlock Holmes audio drama currently awaiting release. He is the author of A Study in Steampunk, the first of Fringeworks' steampunk mash-up novels based on the worls of Sir Arthur Conan Doyle.

LESLEY McINTEE graduated from the University of Manchester in 2011 with an MPhil in German Romanticism and is currently a freelance academic, writer and SciFi convention Chair. She specialises in

19th and 20th century literature, culture, and history of the occult and is currently working on a study of the Brothers Grimm and popular culture for Fringeworks as well as writing in Osprey books' Myth and Legends series. She fits in a day job in retail, and charity fundraising somewhere in the above.

ADRIAN MIDDLETON is a former civil servant and policy adviser on broadband and digital content. He is the publisher and editor of Fringeworks' Moriarty paradigm series and several other books, including the forthcoming anthology, *Holmes vs. Zombies* and *The Scoundrel of Bohemia*, a steampunk mash-up of Conan Doyle's *A Scandal in Bohemia*.

ADEM ROLFE is a rather taciturn freelance author who claims only to have been born on an island somewhere in the North Atlantic. He is the author of *The Lavender Men*, the first original short story to be set within the Moriarty paradigm.

Find out more about Fringeworks by Scanning the QR code below

www.fringeworks.co.uk

ENDNOTE

It should be noted that the articles, *A Note from Doctor Doyle*, and *Some Personalia about myself and Mr. Sherlock Holmes*, are mash-ups loosely based on real pieces written by Conan Doyle. The first is based upon an article published in the Strand Magazine in January 1923, while the second is based upon *Some Personalia about Mr. Sherlock Holmes*, first published in the Strand Magazine in December 1917.

The Moriarty paradigm is a collaborative venture, and the editor of this volume would like to take the opportunity to thank those who have, in some way, contributed towards its gestation.

First, to those authors who have committed to help bring the story to life through a series of novels: David A. McIntee, Mike Chinn, Damon Cavalchini, Jonathan Green, Steve Lockley, Terri Osborne, Jan Edwards and Simon Bucher-Jones. However this series turns out, the end result will be a testament to their contributions and will, I am sure, have a lasting legacy.

Second, to those working with us to bring forward a series of short stories set within the paradigm: Sam Gafford, David Naughton-Shires, Adem Rolfe, Gaie Sebold, Matthew Sylvester and Christer Van;

For the cover, Martin Reimann, Darrel Bevan, Anna Higgins and David R Shires.

For encouragement, research and other forms of assistance too numerous to mention here: Alex Davis, Colin Fisher, Ed Fortune, Stephen Jones, Steve Jones, Jen Leavesley, Lesley McIntee, Nigel Potter, Avril Simister and Neville Watkins;

To those who have inspired us in this project: Guy Adams, Michael Harrison, K. W. Jeter, Andy Lane and, of course, Sir Arthur Conan Doyle.

And finally, to the ones that got away, with whom we hope to work in the future: Raven Dane, Kelly Hale, Michael Kurland and William Meikle.

MORIARTY PARADIGM

ALSO AVAILABLE...

THE SCOUNDREL OF BOHEMIA
by Adrian Middleton

When a masked Count hires Sherlock Holmes to retrieve incriminating evidence, he is plunged into a world of fraud, political intrigue and armed assassins. Will the scoundrel regain his property, or will Miss Adler become the first woman to truly outsmart The great detective. Meanwhile, thirty years earlier, a time traveller arrives in the slums of Old London intent on exacting the most daring masterplan in the history of the British Empire. His name... Professor James Moriarty.

THE LAVENDER MEN
by Adem Rolfe

When Watson is reunited with his loyal wartime orderly, he and Holmes become embroiled in the affairs of the New East India Company. Do dead soldiers fight for the crown? Only by investigating the dark secrets of Limehouse's Medical Ordnance Company can the great detective discover the truth.

A STUDY IN STEAMPUNK
by David A. McIntee

Returning to London to recuperate from injuries sustained over Afghanistan, Dr John Watson's quest for new accommodation brings him face to face with the eccentric Mr Sherlock Holmes, and his consulting rooms at 221B Baker Street. Plunged into the world of the scientific method of detection, the physician finds that he has not, after all, left death and mayhem in his past. He soon finds himself embroiled in a murder mystery involving coded messages, Her Majesty's Aeronautical Service, and the ever-present shadow of Professor James Moriarty. With no shortage of suspects, and the best brains of Scotland Yard left baffled, it is up to the self-styled Consulting Detective, and the recuperating Surgeon-Lieutenant, to learn to work together in unravelling the politics of the People of the Clouds, and to bring to an end an invisible killer's reign of terror.

www.ingramcontent.com/pod-product-compliance
Lightning Source LLC
Chambersburg PA
CBHW060944120626
46557CB00003B/1141